ACROSS

BY
JOHN WILSON

To the students of
Sunshine Hills Elementary

Enjoy
John Wilson
September 10/02.

A·SANDCASTLE·BOOK

An imprint of
Beach Holme Publishing
Vancouver, B.C.

This book is published by Beach Holme Publishing, #226—2040 West 12th Ave., Vancouver, BC, V6J 2G2. This is a Sandcastle Book. A teacher's guide is also available from Beach Holme Publishing at 1-888-551-6655.

The author and publisher acknowledge the generous assistance of The Canada Council and the BC Ministry of Small Business, Tourism and Culture.

THE CANADA COUNCIL | LE CONSEIL DES ARTS
FOR THE ARTS | DU CANADA
SINCE 1957 | DEPUIS 1957

Editor: Joy Gugeler
Cover Art: Barbara Munzar
Production and Design: Teresa Bubela

Canadian Cataloguing in Publication Data:

Wilson, John (John Alexander), 1951-
    Across frozen seas

(A sandcastle book)
ISBN 0-88878-381-7

    1. Northwest Passage--Juvenile fiction. I. Title.
II. Series.

PS8595.I5834A72 1997   jC813',54   C97-900649-X
PZ7.W6959A37 1997

ACROSS FROZEN SEAS

FOR EELIN, WHO TOLD ME STORIES.

PROLOGUE

In the first dream that I remember I am sitting at a long, rough-hewn table with about forty other boys. The table is set in a narrow, dark hall and there are cobwebs hanging from the blackened wooden rafters. At one end, in front of a vast, empty fireplace, sits a large man in a grey uniform of coarse cloth. On the mantle above his head are carved the words, "Work boy or out."

We range in age from five or six (down at the far end of the table) to twelve or fourteen (where I sit). We are all dressed in heavy, woollen clothes that are ragged and often patched at the elbow and the knee. Several boys have flat caps sitting on the table beside them. In front of each boy, including me, is a bowl of thin vegetable soup. We are eating in silence. In fact, there is no sound at all in my dream; I cannot hear or smell, and the soup I am passing up to my mouth has no taste. My only sensations are sight and touch.

The table feels uneven beneath my arm and the soup spoon cold in my hand. I can also feel, clenched in my fist in the warm darkness of my pocket, the small lead figure of a sailor, Jack Tar. He is the only thing I have from my parents and, as long as he is with me, I am certain nothing will go wrong. More acutely, I notice that my backside is extremely tender where it comes in contact with the hard wooden bench.

The whole experience is like watching an old movie, except that I am *in the movie*. I have the distance of a member of the audience and yet I am much more than a passive observer. I am one of the actors. At least I can see through the eyes of one of the actors and feel his pain. I know what he knows, and his past is my past. Although I have never seen this hall or met these children, in my dream everything is very familiar. This place is my home and I feel as if I have been here forever.

I know, beyond a shadow of a doubt, that the man in uniform is called Mister Marback and that, in addition to the large set of brass keys hanging from his belt, he also owns a cane switch he uses on anyone who has broken his rules. This explains the pain in my backside.

The scruffy-looking boy across the table from me is the reason I have felt the brunt of the switch, but I don't seem to mind. He is teaching me to read and write. In fact, it was after candles-out last night, when we were illicitly reading my friend's stolen copy of Mister Dickens' new book *A Christmas Carol*, that Mister Marback caught us. My friend heard him coming an instant before the door opened and slid under the bed, keeping silent while I was beaten. But this injustice doesn't matter; he is my only friend in the world and I would gladly endure this, and more, for him.

My friend is taller than I am and has a mop of sandy-coloured hair that looks as though it has never seen a brush. His face is thin, narrow and unremarkable, except for his eyes. They are deep brown, large and have a droop to the edges, giving his face a sad expression. As I look at him across the table, he lifts his head and smiles at me. Instantly, his eyes come alive and sparkle with mischief. The name *George Chambers* flashes through my mind and I think, *tonight we will escape*.

That was the first dream. Not really anything too unusual, except that I could remember it very vividly the next day. I could even explain it. Two days before, I had been watching the movie *Oliver Twist*. Obviously, the workhouse scene where Oliver asks for a second bowl of gruel had stayed with me and crept into my thoughts that night. There was no hint of the adventure and tragedy that would soon unfold and consume both myself and my dream-friend George.

For a week, I lived my "normal" life. I went to school, played hockey, hung out, got bored and listened to my parents argue. Then I had the second dream.

I am standing in a dark, narrow alley, shivering uncontrollably. It is raining steadily and on either side of me are stained, damp walls. Below my feet are uneven cobblestones that slope toward an open drain. The drain is clogged with garbage and there are puddles of scummy water around it, making me grateful my dream allows no sense of smell. George is about thirty feet ahead of me peering around a corner into a busy roadway. From what little I can see, there appear to be stalls lining both sides of the street and a crush of people dressed in the same old-fashioned clothes as the boys in my first dream. I want to go closer and look, but George has told me to stay back. Without hesitation, he slips around the corner and out of sight.

In a moment he returns, running as fast as he can. In each hand he holds a coarse, brown loaf of bread. As he runs past he laughs and tosses me one of the loaves. In that instant, an older boy rounds the corner into the alley and begins running towards us. He is not much taller than I am but he looks angry. Frightened, I turn to follow George, but my foot slips on the slick cobblestones and I fall. The loaf of bread slides from my grasp into a foul black puddle. Before I can get up the boy is on me, holding my collar and hitting the back of my head with his other fist. I try to put my hands behind my head to protect myself, but he keeps on hitting. His blows hurt and I am crying. Without warning, the awful smell coming from the filthy water only a couple of inches from my nose wells up and overwhelms me. It is like nothing I have ever smelled before and it makes my empty stomach heave.

Abruptly, the hitting stops, the hand lets go of my collar, and I fall to the ground and scramble away from the disgusting drain. When I turn over, I see George. He is tearing into the bigger boy like a whirlwind, punching and kicking furiously. The boy is trying to hit back, but George's head is down and the blows bounce harmlessly off his back. George's punches, on the other hand, are finding their mark and the boy is being steadily forced back toward the street. Eventually, he gives up and runs around the corner. George turns back toward me. He is out of breath, but grinning as if he has enjoyed every minute. His loaf of bread is still clutched protectively under one arm. I pull myself up and look disconsolately at the soggy, inedible mass that used to be my loaf. As George draws level, he breaks off a piece of his loaf and passes it to me. We turn and walk off down the alley, George talking happily while I munch hungrily on the bread. It tastes bitter, but it is the only food I have had in days and I wolf it down.

I awoke puzzled. This dream was obviously related to the one I had had a week before. It had the same vividness and the same feeling of being trapped inside someone else's head. I had heard of people having the same dream repeated over and over again, but the idea of having a sequence of dreams, where each continues the action from the one before (like a television series), was bizarre. Even stranger, I felt as if I were being drawn more and more deeply into the dream world, whatever, and whenever, that was. Now that I could smell and taste, the only missing sense was hearing.

Equally odd, although I hadn't dreamt it, I somehow knew what had happened to my dream self and George between the two dreams. He and I had indeed escaped the night after the first dream. I remembered squeezing myself through a tiny window into a dark alley and running until I could hardly draw another breath into my aching lungs.

After that, George and I had lived on the streets, stealing what food we could and sleeping wherever we could find some shelter. It was always raining. Our only happiness was the stolen copy of *A Christmas Carol* which George and I, huddled beneath a bridge, would read to one another. My reading was still very slow and George often had to help me, but we both loved the escape into Scrooge's world of ghosts and Christmas turkey. Our favourite bit was the description of the ghost of Christmas Present, surrounded by piles of food and gifts. We would torture ourselves by reading of the "great joints of meat," "long wreaths of sausages," and "seething bowls of punch," until our stomachs were growling so loudly we couldn't continue.

How I knew all this without actually dreaming it was a mystery. Yet, somehow, I did, and what's more, I was beginning to care about what happened to my dreaming self. I found myself anxious to go to sleep the next night so that the story could continue.

CHAPTER 1

The next night I sat in my small room in our house in Humboldt, Saskatchewan fingering an old ivory button. On one side was a carved crown and anchor and, scratched on the other, a broad arrow which identified it as having come from the uniform of a sailor in the British Navy. I often sat and looked at it. The button fascinated me. Who wore it? How had he lost it? An ancestor of my grandfather Jim's had found it on an expedition to the Canadian Arctic years ago. He said the owner must have died long before I was even born, but it seemed now as if a part of that sailor were still alive. When I held his button in my hand he was not alone and neither was I.

As for being alone, I don't have brothers or sisters, so I'm used to spending time in my room by myself, just thinking. When I was younger, I used to wish for a brother to play with, but now I can amuse myself for hours thinking about where I'll go when I leave home.

Often my mother interrupts my thoughts with her worried knocks at the door asking, "David Young, what *can* you be doing in there?" I usually reply, "Homework," and then go back to my plans for the future.

In the meantime, I play hockey and hang out, and in the summer I canoe and fish, but that's about all there is to do. Humboldt is definitely not a thriving city. It's a small town about fifty kilometres east of Saskatoon and about as many years behind the rest of the world. As soon as I'm old enough, I'm gone. My friends are always talking about Toronto or Vancouver, but I'm heading north. As far north as I can get. Maybe I'll get hired by a government survey or work on the rigs; I'd take any job in order to get up there. If I want to stay though, I suppose I'll have to go to college first and learn a trade that will be useful in the North.

The Arctic has always fascinated me. I like the idea of the white wilderness, and of living on the edge of the world. Humboldt's not quite the edge of the world, but I like the winters here too, especially the storms when the snow whips across the prairie with nothing to stop it but the occasional grain elevator. Nothing matters to the snow—cars, roads, houses—it covers everything in its path, smoothes it over. Even sound is trapped by the falling flakes. Then it gets cold, minus twenty, thirty, even forty degrees sometimes, but then the sun comes out and the air gets so clear you can see forever. When it's that cold, your nose tingles when you breathe and the snow is crisp and dry under your feet. Mom says that when I was younger, I used to sit at the window and watch the snow fall for hours. I still like to watch those big flakes drift down, thousands and thousands of them blanketing the silent land.

When it's snowing you feel as though you could be anywhere. They say no two snowflakes are the same, yet the ones that fall today are identical to those that fell on the huge ice sheet that once covered the prairie, or those that fell on the hairy backs of the mammoths in prehistoric times, or those that settled on bundles of beaver pelts the fur traders carried along the river ways. I love thinking about the past and, somehow, the snow is a link; it feels the same to everyone, regardless of when they lived or died.

All this I have learned from my grandpa Jim, Mom's father, who lives on a farm about ten kilometres out of town. His story began when his parents came over from England at the turn of the century, before Saskatchewan was even a province. They didn't know anything about farming, but I guess things were bad enough where they came from to make them want to leave and take a chance on Canada. Jim has a photograph of them, taken in their first year here, standing in front of a ramshackle sod cabin dressed in their city clothes with high, stiff collars and fancy hats. They *did* manage to make a go of it; the farm did surprisingly well, even through the depression years.

Jim was the second of two brothers. Both were born around the time of the First World War and both went off to fight in the Second. Jim was in a tank that was attacked in Holland at the end of the war. He was lucky; he was the only one who got out alive. He has limped ever since due to a piece of shrapnel embedded in his hip. His brother was not so lucky. He was a spitfire pilot who shot down dozens of enemy planes. One day he took off on a routine patrol and disappeared. No one ever found out what happened to him. He must have crashed into the sea.

After his wound healed, Jim came back to Saskatchewan and took over the farm. He married a local woman named Elly, and my Mom was their only child. I think they were a little disappointed when Mom married my father and moved to town. Dad's not a farmer, so there is no one left to take over the farm. I suppose it will be sold when Jim dies. Elly died six years ago, but Jim is still there. He's too old to do any of the work now so most of the land is rented out. Last fall, Jim found even working around the yard too much, so he hired a Hutterite boy named Jurgen who lives on a farm across the road. I've never met him, but Jim says he's a hard worker and good company.

I imagine Jim tells Jurgen his stories. Jim has always been a great storyteller, and he even loves the Arctic as much as I do. His ancestor, the one who found the button, was a sailor on an expedition to the Arctic in the 1850's. They went north to find out what had happened to Franklin and his men on an expedition to the area ten years earlier. Franklin was trying to find the Northwest Passage to China, but they never reached their destination and all the sailors and both their ships disappeared just as strangely as Jim's brother had.

Jim's ancestor didn't unearth much except bones and Inuit stories, but he did bring back some relics: spoons, knives, bits of wood and rope. Most of them are in museums now, except for my button. But we still don't know much about what happened to Franklin.

Jim also told me stories of other explorers: Charles Francis Hall, who lived with the Inuit for five years; Schwatka, the cavalry officer, who covered five thousand kilometres by sled; and De Long, who died on the coast of Russia because his men couldn't make the locals understand that he was starving to death nearby. And, Jim said, at the other end of the world, there were Scott, Shackleton and Amundsen racing to reach the south pole. Jim tells great stories, so great that I often used to sit by the fire in his living room for hours, listening to him talk while the snow fell outside.

I don't seem to have time for stories any more, but they have left me with a love of the North and the certainty that one day I will go there and see it for myself. But for now, I will have to be content with this button, Jim's stories, and my dreams.

CHAPTER 2

I am cold, wet, hungry and miserable. We are standing
on a grey street under a leaden sky. In front of us, steps
lead up to an imposing, carved wooden door. I am
looking around and through the haze of my dream I
think, *perhaps the cars will give me a clue as to the year.* But
there are no cars to be seen. The street is cobbled and
the only transportation visible is a black, polished
coach. It sits on two wheels almost as large as I am and
is drawn by a single brown horse. A driver sits at the
back, guiding the reins over the roof and, as the vehicle
passes, I catch a glimpse of the white faces of two
passengers inside. I turn back to the door. George is
saying something and, almost before I realize it, we are
climbing the steps. I stand back while my friend raises
the brass, lion's-head knocker.

After a moment, the door opens and a woman in a
maid's costume looks out. She is obviously unimpressed
by the sight of us. George is moving into the open

doorway and talking fast, but not fast enough. With a look of utter disgust, the maid slams the door in his face. I can't really blame her. We must look pretty scruffy after living on the streets for two weeks. Turning, we slump dejectedly down on the step. Now, how will we get in to see Sir John, the naval hero, the talk of all London, and our only chance to go to sea?

I shiver in the damp air and pull Jack Tar out of my pocket. He is a lead figure, only about three inches tall, dressed in a bright blue sailor's uniform with white trim and a hand capped over his eyes. He gazes into the distance at some far-off shore, just as George and I had hoped to do. Will I ever get to see the things he has seen, or am I destined only to look out on the damp, rainy back streets of London?

Jack Tar is still in my hand twenty minutes later when a carriage pulls up in front of us. It is larger than most of the others that have gone by, with four wheels and two horses. A footman, who has been riding on the back, jumps down and holds the door open for an elderly, heavy-set man with the largest ears I have ever seen. He is wearing an impressive dark blue uniform with two rows of buttons down the front. The shoulders are decorated with gold epaulettes and he is wearing heavy-looking medals on his right breast and at his throat. His hat is like the ones you see in the old pictures of Admiral Nelson, peaked and triangular with a tassel of gold braid. In his left hand, he carries a thin gold baton.

The uniform is crumpled and a couple of the brass

buttons are unfastened, making it look as if he has slept, or at least dozed, in it. His face is heavy set but does not look healthy. The skin is pasty white and there are bags under both eyes. The eyes themselves look watery and bloodshot.

As I watch in confusion, the man takes a hesitant step forward, throws back his head, closes his eyes and lets out an enormous sneeze. I cannot hear it, but even several feet away, I can see his body convulse and spit fly from his open mouth. His baton falls to the ground and rolls toward an open drain. Instinctively, I recoil, but George is more alert. Before the footman can even move, he darts down the steps and retrieves the golden stick so it doesn't fall down the open hole. Looking small, George stands before the gentleman and offers him the rescued baton. He peers at George from behind the folds of an enormous white handkerchief.

Finally, the footman reacts. Brushing past his master, he grabs the baton from George and catches hold of my friend's collar. Never one to take an attack lying down, George reacts by landing a swift kick to the footman's shin which makes the man cry out in pain. However, it doesn't make him loosen his grip and George remains a prisoner. But not for long.

"Unhand the boy. He's done nothing wrong." The great man draws himself upright and glares sternly at the footman.

"But Sir John..." the footman protests. With a wave of his hand and a ghost of a smile on his sickly face, Sir John steps forward and unclasps the footman's hand from George's threadbare jacket. Realizing his rescuer is Sir John himself, George immediately begins talking. He explains who we are and why we are here. Sir John listens with a slightly amused expression on his face. Behind him, another carriage rumbles noisily past on the uneven cobblestones.

"So, you want to go to sea?" Sir John's voice is hoarse from his cold. For the first time, he looks over at me. I try to stand straight in what I assume to be the proper military manner. His eyes linger on me and then drift to Jack Tar on the step beside me.

"I see we shall get two sailors for the price of one with you my lad." Sir John smiles and, in spite of his cold, his face turns gentle. "I was your age when I fought with Nelson at the battle of Copenhagen, and I was not much older at Trafalgar." For a moment, he seems on the verge of drifting off into the past. With visible effort he pulls himself back.

"The world is changing my boy. Only this morning I was getting one of those new-fangled Daguerreotype pictures made. Don't hold with them myself. I much prefer a good old-fashioned painted portrait, but they tell me this new method is more accurate and will last forever. Long after I'm dead people will see my face fixed on a glass plate. Trouble is, I've got this terrible cold. Is that how I want people to remember me, with a red nose and puffy cheeks? Hah! At least a painter could make me look decent."

His watery eyes swing away from me and back to George.

"I'll see what I can do," he says. Then, turning to the footman, "Take these boys around to the kitchen and see that they get a good square meal."

With a mumbled "thank you," George and I follow the footman to the side of the house and through a much less imposing door. As soon as we cross the threshold we are hit by a blast of warm air. The kitchen is huge and smells of smoke and wet laundry and food. The laundry is hanging from a system of pulleys drawn up close to the high ceiling. The floor is made of flagstones and the only furnishings are a large wooden table and bench sitting in the middle of the room. One entire wall is taken up with a long, black, iron range and a variety of pots and pans. In front of the range, two women are stirring something in the pots. They turn as we come in and the footman speaks.

"These 'ere ragamuffins seems to 'ave taken Sir John's fancy. See that they gets sommat to eat."

The accent is heavy and strange, but we don't hear any more as the footman turns on his heel and leaves. One of the women comes over and starts fussing with our clothes.

"Millie, the poor mites is soaking! 'elp me get these things off 'em and give us some o' that stew 'ere."

Before we know it, we are sitting at the table wrapped in coarse blankets eating the most delicious meal I have ever tasted while our clothes steam above us. It is such a luxury to be warm and dry and well fed. Neither of us speak. We are too engrossed in the feast before us. I have almost finished my third plateful when a door in the corner by the range opens and a tall man in black enters. The two women, who have been chattering, fall silent as he crosses the room and, to my horror, addresses me.

"Can you read boy?" he asks in a sombre voice.

"A little," I reply with a nervous stutter.

"Well then," he continues, "take this to the address on the front and give it to the gentleman you find there."

I nod dumbly as he hands me an envelope. On the front, in beautiful curled handwriting, is a name, James Fitzjames, and an address. The back is sealed with wax bearing the impression of a crown and anchor. The tall man leaves and, almost instinctively, I hand the envelope to George. He looks excited.

"This is it," he says triumphantly looking down at the piece of sealed paper in his hand. "This is what we came for. This'll get us into the Navy, maybe even on Sir John's own ship!" He looks up at me. "We're going to have *some* adventures now, Davy boy!"

CHAPTER 3

My first thought on waking up after the third dream was, "I can hear." And so I could. I had heard the voices of Sir John, the footman, the cooks and, most importantly, my friend George. My dreams were becoming more real. *I was beginning to be a part of them.* The feeling of happiness I had felt at the kitchen table with the endless supply of food before me lingered on as I lay in my bed that morning. I had never been so happy. The warmth, the food, the friendship had all been so real and immediate that I missed them now that I was awake. For the first time since they had begun, I wished I were back in my dreams.

I knew now I had been in London, England, but when? Who was James Fitzjames? What was Sir John about to do? I began to think back over my dreams. What clues did I have? Obviously, my dream world was a long time ago. There were no cars, only horse-drawn carriages, and the clothes and language were antiquated.

Then it came to me. Jumping out of bed, I ran over to where my school books lay in a disorganized heap. There was one there from my English class that might help. It gave short biographies of all the famous authors we had to read. I turned to the page that listed:

"Dickens, Charles (1812-1870)

...*A Christmas Carol* was one of a series of
Christmas stories that Dickens wrote. First
published in 1844 it became an instant
popular success...."

The book George and I loved to read on the streets was a stolen, new copy of *A Christmas Carol*. My dream world must be set in the winter of 1844/45. But why?

There was one more clue I could follow. Sir John was a famous figure in London at that time. Without a surname it would be difficult to look him up, but there was one person who might be able to help me— Jim. He knew a lot about the history of that time and he had all kinds of books we could look through.

For two nights I went to bed in a turmoil of excitement hoping for the next dream, but none came. Each morning I would wake up feeling empty after a long, dreamless sleep. Finally, on Saturday, I took the bus along Highway 5 to Jim's place. It was one of those great February days when the air feels like crystal. It was about minus twenty-five degrees, but the sun was shining brightly and the snow looked as if someone had sprinkled handfuls of diamonds over it. I was wearing my parka, so I was warm enough while I walked along the gravel road.

Jim's farm is about two kilometres off the highway. It sits across the gravel road from the Hutterite farm where Jurgen lives. The Hutterites are descended from European religious refugees who came to Canada to escape persecution. They settled all over the prairies in colonies, housing up to one hundred people. They keep pretty much to themselves and still dress in hand-made clothes. They work hard and their farms are very efficiently run.

One time Jim took me down to visit them. That was when he was first thinking of getting one of the boys to do chores for him. When we got there, all the kids came out to see us. They rarely leave the property as all the schooling is done on the farm, so they were keen to see outsiders. They didn't act like kids from the city. They just stood around us in silence and stared. The boys stood in the front and the girls stood behind. I said "Hi," and waved, but they didn't move. Then some of the elders arrived. They knew Jim and started talking. Their words were strange and old-fashioned, with lots of "thou's" and "thee's," and their accents were strong. Jim said it was because they still speak medieval German among themselves.

Jim talked with the elders for some time. He said afterwards that they weren't keen on letting someone off the farm. The only chance boys get to leave is to go to another settlement to work when they are teenagers. There, they get menial work, but they can meet other people and often marry and settle down. When a settlement gets too big, a group will split off and go and set up a new farm somewhere else.

The elders finally let someone go because Jim's place was close by and because he had known them for a long time. The Hutterites interested me and I wanted to get to know Jurgen, but he had not been at Jim's on the few occasions I had visited recently.

The first thing you see at Jim's place is the mailbox. There's a carved and painted squirrel on top with a hole in its back where Elly used to put flowers in the summer. I think it looks pretty hokey, and I guess Jim does too, because there haven't been flowers in it since Elly died, but then, he hasn't taken it down either.

The farmhouse is about fifty metres off the road, surrounded by a rundown barn and corrals. There's even an old sty from a time when Jim kept pigs. They're all empty now. A Jersey cow called Victoria lives in the barn. She's long past the age of giving milk, but Jim keeps her as a kind of companion on the farm. Even in winter, he spends long hours sitting with Victoria remembering the past. Apart from Victoria in the barn, the old farmyard is dead. Life is concentrated around the new barn and the corrals down the hill on the land that is rented by one of Jim's neighbours.

Jim took a while to answer my ring. He can't move around too quickly any more, but we were soon sitting at his kitchen table drinking hot chocolate. I had convinced myself that as soon as I found the answer to who Sir John was, my dreams would continue. The excitement of the past few days was too much and I blurted out the story of my dreams so far.

Jim listened with interest, nodding occasionally. When I mentioned Sir John and Fitzjames he looked puzzled. I finished by telling him how I thought the dreams were set in the winter of 1844/45. For what seemed like a long time, we sat in silence at the table, me in an agony of anticipation, Jim deep in thought.

"Well," I asked eventually, unable to contain myself any longer. "Do you know what's happening? Who is Sir John?"

Jim looked up, then slowly rose and fetched a book from the parlour. It was hardcover and looked quite old. Carefully, he laid it on the table between us and opened it to the collection of photographs in the centre. One was of a rather jovial man in an old-fashioned uniform. He was holding a hat in his left hand and a large brass telescope in his right. Underneath, the caption read:

"Commander James Fitzjames—Captain, H.M.S. *Erebus*."

"That's the guy in my dream!" I said, more loudly than I had intended. "Who is he?"

"*Was* he," corrected Jim. "H.M.S. *Erebus* and H.M.S. *Terror* were ships of an expedition that went to the Arctic in the 1840's."

"The time's right," I interrupted. "What did they do?"

Jim paused and looked thoughtfully at me for a long moment.

"They all died," he said finally.

The words seemed to hang in the air between us. Again it was Jim who broke the silence.

"The expedition was led by a man who, as a youth, fought at Trafalgar and went on to become a famous Arctic explorer. His name was Sir John Franklin."

The Franklin Expedition! The doomed men that Jim's ancestor had gone in search of! My dream character must have been trying to join them. Slowly, Jim turned to the previous page. There he was! Sir John, just as I remembered—the big ears, and an imposing uniform with the two buttons undone. Even in this grainy image, his nose looked swollen and his eyes were puffy. Sir John Franklin, on the very day I met him in my dream. *What does it mean?*

I hadn't realized that I had spoken out loud until Jim answered my last question.

"I don't know," he said, looking at me oddly. "I thought you had forgotten all those old stories I told you."

"No, I haven't," I replied, "and anyway, you never told me Franklin's first name or that he had a cold when his picture was taken. And what about George? Who is he? And all the details about London? How could I know all that?"

"I don't know. You used to read a lot. Perhaps bits from old books are coming back to you. The mind can work in very strange ways."

"It's not my imagination," I interrupted. "These dreams are real. They are telling me things I couldn't possibly have known. Something strange is happening."

Jim looked at me seriously for a minute.

"Is everything all right at school? At home?"

I was hurt. Jim thought I was imagining it all! I had come for two reasons. I had hoped Jim could answer my questions, but I also hoped he would listen, understand, and help me figure out what was going on. But, instead, he was dismissing what I said as a bad dream brought on by stress or bad grades.

I mumbled an excuse about having to get back home and left. The walk back to the road was much longer and colder than on the way out. I began to kick myself for leaving so quickly. Jim was just trying to help. But what bothered me was that he had struck a nerve. Things were *not* going well at home. Mom and Dad had been arguing a lot recently and were so wrapped up in their own worries that they had even less time for me. I didn't want to tell Jim about Mom and Dad's fights; he didn't need to worry too.

When I got back to town I got out my skates and went down to the rink to shoot the puck around, but my heart wasn't in it and I soon gave up. As the day wore on I became more restless. What I had learned from Jim was always in my mind. I wasn't tired, but I went to bed early and forced myself to go to sleep. Maybe tonight....

CHAPTER 4

The docks and embankments along the Thames River are lined with cheering people. Flags are flying everywhere and the harbour is full of little boats. The air is thick with music and the sound of horns. The bright spring sun glistens off the rows of medals on the chests of those who have come to see us off. Sir James Ross is here, as well as Colonel Edward Sabine of the Royal Society. Amid the chaos, our two ships are almost lost.

It is 10:30 on the morning of Monday the 19th of May, 1845 and we are setting off on our great adventure. There is not one person watching who expects anything but for us to return to a hero's welcome in a year or two. We will complete the Northwest Passage and be the first ships to sail around the top of the world. This should not be a difficult task. After all, there is only a sixty mile stretch of the passage unexplored along the coast of King William Land. We will collect a vast amount of invaluable scientific information, from detailed magnetic readings to specimens of every type of plant, rock and animal we come across. We will surpass the achievements of James Ross and William Parry with this single exploit. We have the best ships, the most experienced crews and the best provisions ever to have been dedicated to an Arctic voyage. How can we possibly fail?

The *Erebus* leads the way through the throng of smaller vessels. She is not large and looks decidedly squat compared to some of the sleek yachts that have come to see us off. The mountains of equipment and supplies piled on her decks only add to this impression. Osmer, the purser, is standing behind me talking animatedly to anyone who will listen. As always, his conversation consists of little more than a list of the supplies we have on board. I have heard it a dozen times before: sixty tons of flour, thirty tons of salt meat, four tons of chocolate, three tons of tobacco, a ton each of tea, soap and candles, eight thousand cans of meat, soup and vegetables, over three thousand gallons of liquor, and ten live oxen. To prevent the dreaded scurvy, we also have over nine hundred gallons of lemon juice and one hundred seventy gallons of cranberries. We shall certainly eat well, but of greater interest to me are the seventeen hundred books in the ship's library. They shall feed my mind in the long hours of Arctic winter darkness.

Perhaps as important as the supplies we carry is the experience and knowledge contained in the heads of our officers and crew. Sir John, of course, has spent as long in the Arctic as any man alive save the native inhabitants of the region. Captain Crozier on the *Terror* has been north twice before and speaks the local language passably well. He also commanded the *Terror* under Sir James Ross in the Antarctic. Lieutenant Gore was mate on the *Terror* when she went north and Osmer himself was up there twenty years ago. The ice masters and many of our crew know well what we are getting into from their time on whaling ships searching the waters of Baffin Bay.

Both our ships are strong and well suited for the journey. They began life as bomb ships carrying mortars that were used to bombard coastal fortresses during the wars against Napoleon. For this work they had to be broad and their timbers had to be heavily reinforced. They have been further reinforced and covered with iron sheeting to withstand the Arctic ice. We also have steam engines to help navigate through the ice. Below the black funnel jutting through the *Erebus'* deck sits an entire railway engine with only the wheels missing. This will provide us with power when there is no wind. The cold will be held at bay by a system of pipes that carry hot water and steam from a small boiler to the rest of the ship. Fresh water is made from sea water in a new apparatus attached to the galley stoves.

As the *London Times* newspaper stated but one week ago, "The Lords Commissioners of the Admiralty have, in every respect, provided most liberally for the comforts of the officers and men of an expedition which may, with the...advantages of modern science, be attended with great results."

All these men look resplendent in their uniforms adorned with glittering medals and honours, but they are eclipsed by the figure standing a few feet from me. Sir John has no cold now and he looks positively regal standing on the quarter deck of the *Erebus* acknowledging the cheers of the crowd with a wave of his gold baton. Beside him stands Fitzjames, looking almost too young, despite his receding hairline, to be captain of such a ship. He has never been to the Arctic, but he has experience of ships and men. Just three years ago, he was leading a rocket brigade in China and he was on the first expedition to navigate the Euphrates River. Today, his round face is wreathed in smiles as he quietly gives the orders which will take us down the river to the open ocean.

Of course, George and I are not up there among the officers. We stand on the main deck among the common sailors and marines. Weeks have passed since we stood shivering on Sir John's doorstep. We have been assigned to the same duties aboard the *Erebus*. As I will soon be twelve and George is fourteen, we are cabin boys, although some of the sailors are not much older than George. I am amazed how fast I have learned the Navy routine. All it seems to require is silence in the presence of officers and a rapid and unquestioning obedience to orders. It is hard work, but we are well fed and it is paradise compared to living on the streets.

Now all the preparation is over and we are off.

Amid all the confusion, my attention settles on Neptune, the ship's dog. He is large, brown, and very companionable. He is one of two pets on board, the other being a trained monkey called Jacko. Neptune seems to me to be the only one here not happy with the proceedings. He is sitting in a corner gazing mournfully around at the bustling crowd. He does not seem pleased to be accompanying us, although he has been on other voyages and is said to enjoy them greatly. Perhaps the occasion is too much for him. My thoughts are interrupted by George touching my arm. He points up.

"Look," he says, "a dove on the masthead. It is the bird of peace and harmony—a good omen."

An omen to confirm what we all feel to be true. What luck we have to be a part of such an adventure. I cannot imagine being happier.

Icebergs glitter all around us in the midnight sun. Yesterday I counted eighty-five. I have not yet mastered the art of sleeping in a hammock, so I have come up on deck to get some air. Yesterday, July 12, 1845, we left Disco on the coast of Greenland after taking aboard the last of our supplies and saying farewell to our supply ship, the *Barretto Junior* under Lieutenant Griffiths. Our decks are now stacked even higher with coal and crates and we sit very low in the water. We slaughtered the ten oxen we brought up with us and shall have our last fresh meat until we reach the other side of the world.

"It is quite wonderful, is it not?"

I am startled by the soft voice beside me. Turning I see Mister Fitzjames leaning on the rail. Hurriedly I stand at attention. "Aye sir," I answer.

"Stand easy boy," Fitzjames smiles slightly and turns to look back over the ice. "It is too much of an adventure to waste in sleep, I think. They say the spring is early this year and we shall have an easy passage across Baffin Bay. Perhaps one season might even see our journey complete. I hope not. I have an urge to spend a winter in the ice and it would be a great opportunity to take the magnetic readings commissioned by the Royal Society."

All the while, Mister Fitzjames is gazing over the side of the ship and talking to the dark water. His reverie is broken as six sleek shapes break the surface beside us and leap forward in a halo of bright phosphorescence.

"Porpoise," he says happily. "A good omen for us." He turns to face me. "Keep your eyes open and watch everything young lad. Sir John has charged us with examining all we see, from a flea to a whale, and giving our opinion of it. No one has come this way as well equipped to study this land as we, and I feel we will be remembered for what we do here many years after we return.

"What is your name?"

"Davy, sir," I reply haltingly.

"Well Davy," he continues, looking at me keenly, "what do your parents think of you coming on this adventure with us?"

"My parents are dead sir," I reply. "It was the cholera."

"Oh. I'm sorry," he says tilting his head and gazing back at the icebergs. "Mine are too. They died when I was seven. I was taken in by my uncle, but he is dead some years ago. The Navy is my family now.

"Perhaps it will be yours as well," he says, looking back at me. "It doesn't matter what your beginnings are, it is what you do with what you have that counts. Life in the Navy is hard, but there is no feeling on earth like that of sailing into some exotic port beneath palm-covered hills and a tropical sky."

His smile broadens.

"But we must have this adventure first, and I fear we shall see precious few palm trees in the next year or two."

Fitzjames pauses and his gaze drifts over to the red sun low on the western horizon.

"Well," he continues, "it is late. I must bid you good-night. Sleep well lad."

As I watch Fitzjames return to his cabin, I reach into my pocket and clutch Jack Tar. Silently, the icebergs slip by like snowy mountain peaks adrift on glass. This is the adventure I always dreamed of.

CHAPTER 5

That morning I lay awake for the longest time, savouring the lingering feeling of the dream. Everything was so unbelievably fresh and new. I was a part of something so thrilling that having to step out of that world and back into my own left a knot in the pit of my stomach.

As I lay in bed going over the details of our send-off and my conversation with Fitzjames, I thought about being alone. I always had friends at school and I went to parties, but I was never really close to anyone. I was just as happy sitting on my own, reading. I used to love escaping into an adventure story that took me to a different world. It could be a different planet, or a different time, or a fantasy world. It didn't matter as long as I could escape. Sometimes, if I was reading a really good story, I would read until midnight or one in the morning and have the hardest time getting up for school. The following day would be a blur, but as soon as I got home I would be back into the book again. It was getting to be like that now. I had only just woken up and yet I was already looking forward to the next night's dreams.

But there was something I *could* do to fill my waking time—I could learn about the actual Franklin expedition. Jim had given me a start, but I was sure there was more I could discover. So I haunted the local library. It didn't offer much, but there were a couple of general books and the staff could order more from Saskatoon. I read everything I could get about Franklin and his men. I read about his earlier expeditions and I read about the expeditions sent to look for him. I read about James Ross reaching the Magnetic Pole, and William Parry being the first man to successfully winter his crew in the High Arctic. I read the journals of men who had been on the Arctic ships. Some of these accounts were not very readable. Others transported me to the world of their authors. More than once, I was struck by the fact that I was reading the very books that were in the library of the *Erebus*, books read by my dream self.

I became an expert on the Franklin expedition. Not that there was a vast amount of concrete information to become an expert on, but what I did learn confirmed what I had dreamt. The *Erebus*, the *Terror*, and their crews had indeed set off to sail through the Northwest Passage in May of 1845. Then they disappeared.

For a long time no one back in England worried. The expedition was well supplied and was expected to last several years. Less prepared crews had spent three or four winters in the Arctic with no loss of life. However, people became concerned when no word had been received from the expedition by 1848. Search ships were sent out, but it wasn't until 1850 that traces of Franklin and his men were finally found. These consisted of discarded equipment, cairns and the foundations of several buildings on Beechey Island, where the expedition had spent its first winter in 1845-46. Three graves also marked the spot. In succeeding years, Inuit stories were heard of large groups of white men struggling across the Arctic and, later, of camps surrounded by bodies.

This was enough evidence for the British government, who did not want to spend more money on a fruitless search, but Franklin's wife was more determined. Lady Jane Franklin harried and badgered the stuffy politicians to make them find out what had happened to her husband. When she couldn't get them to do anything more, she resolved to unearth the answer herself.

In 1857, she financed a private expedition under Captain Francis McClintock. This was the expedition on which Jim's ancestor collected the Naval button. In the spring of 1859, McClintock explored the coast of King William Island (it was called King William Land in those days) by sled. He found many relics including an abandoned boat-sled containing skeletons. Most dramatically, he found the only written record of Franklin and his men. It was in a cairn at Victory Point close to where both the *Erebus* and *Terror* were trapped in the ice over the winters of 1846-47 and 1847-48. It consisted of two messages. The first was written in May, 1847 and had been deposited by Lieutenant Gore as he set off to explore King William Island and complete the last unknown stretch of the Northwest Passage. It ended with a cheerful "All well."

The second note was written in the margin, around the first, and was dated April 25, 1848. By this time Franklin and Gore were both dead and Crozier was leading the one hundred five survivors away from the ships. Many relics and bodies were found scattered along the coast of King William Island and on the Adelaide Peninsula where, several years later, the final resting place of a large party of Franklin's men was discovered at Starvation Cove. Based on this evidence, it was assumed that all the men died in 1848 in the attempt to escape south to a Hudson's Bay post.

Other traces were found over the years. As recently as 1993, the remains of eleven of Franklin's crewmen were found on the barren shores of King William Island, but nothing that contradicted the early accounts. Inuit stories were told to explorers as late as the 1920's, and though these were detailed, they were often confused in poor translation. They did not always support the generally accepted view, but were usually ignored where they didn't match. The Inuit told of finding large quantities of paper with writing on it, but it was considered of no importance and given to the children to play with. No one ever found the ships or any other written record of what had happened.

More recently, studies of the bodies buried on Beechey Island have suggested that the canned food on board the ships was contaminated with lead and that this poisoned some of the crew. Since only a portion of the expedition's food was canned, it is not possible to say what effect this had on the fate of the group as a whole.

All this information was in the books I read on Arctic exploration. After I had finished four or five, it was all so familiar that I began to almost believe that Jim had been right when he said I was remembering things I had read long ago. Maybe my waking mind had simply forgotten the details which were stored in my subconscious, feeding my dreams. But I didn't really believe it. The dreams were *too* detailed, *too* vivid.

What upset me most was reading the accounts of finding the pitiful relics scattered along the bleak shoreline. It sent chills down my spine. Was this how my dreams would end? Were George and my dream-self destined to starve or freeze beneath a canvas tent or under some upturned boat? I didn't know, but I had to find out.

Every night I would escape into a world of my own, driven by the urge to know what happened next. Every night I went to sleep in a fever of expectation. I was not often disappointed.

CHAPTER 6

It is like we are going through a gate to another world. On the horizon, on both sides of our ships, lie snow-capped peaks sitting atop black, wave-washed cliffs. The air is crystal, the sea calm and dotted with gleaming ice floes. The crew are crowding the masts to catch a glimpse of this new world we have come to explore. Even Neptune seems happy.

We have not had the easy crossing of Baffin Bay that Mister Fitzjames hoped for. The winds and the ice have held us back and for weeks we have had to tack back and forth through the towering icebergs. At the end of July we met with two whaling vessels, the *Prince of Wales* and the *Enterprise*. We anchored to a large iceberg and used the time for celestial observation. Sir John and the other officers exchanged visits and many of the crew shouted messages across as some of the whalers knew each other from earlier voyages to these waters. After several days of pleasant company the wind changed and we completed our crossing to Lancaster Sound, the beginning of the fabled Northwest Passage. We expect to see no one else until we sail around Alaska. We are now alone: one hundred twenty-nine men, two ships and enough food for at least four years. We are happy now, but how will we feel by the time we reach the other end?

"Well, we're doing it Davy boy!" George is as jubilant as the rest of the crew. "This is a better life than old Marback's workhouse, eh?"

I nod. It's true; the fresh air, the companionship, the regular food, even double pay for Arctic service...I would not have believed any of this possible only a few months ago. Most importantly, for the first time in six years, I feel like I belong.

The summer I turned six, my parents died. I remember little of them; my mother doing chores, my father sitting in his armchair reading the newspaper. It's evening and my father has just returned from work. He's tired, but he beckons me over to sit on his knee.

"Do you know what today is?" he asks.

"No sir," I reply, aware only that it must be something special.

"Today," he continues, "you are six. Quite a young man, so I have brought you a present."

With that he produces a small package from behind his back. The only presents I remember receiving were small wooden toys and, last Christmas, a carved boat. This is obviously something different.

"Go on, open it," my mother encourages.

Almost reverently, I unwrap the small box and remove the lid. There, lying on a bed of crushed paper is Jack Tar. He gleams, bright in his freshly-painted uniform. He is turned slightly to the side and holds one hand up to shield the sun from his eyes as he looks off to a distant horizon. He is the most beautiful thing I have ever seen. Barely able to say thank you, I slide to the floor and begin the first of many games with him.

Two months later, cholera sweeps through London and both my parents are dead. I am about to begin a different life in institutions and "homes." Some orphanages are good and some are bad, but none make me feel like I belong the way I did on that long ago birthday. Now, with George and my shipmates beside me, I feel that way again. I put my hand in my pocket and protectively clutch Jack Tar.

"Yes, George," I reply as he puts his arm over my shoulder, "we have been very lucky."

"Lucky! Lucky nothing. We *made* it all happen. We ran away. We lived on the streets. We found Sir John. We did it all."

This is typical of George. His parents abandoned him as a baby and he lived his entire life (except for a period with some charitable ladies who taught him to read and write) either on the streets or in the work-house. Since we first met, over two years ago, he has been the leader and always planned our escapes.

The numbing drudgery of the workhouse was often no worse than the empty-bellied freedom of living on the streets. Marback's was the worst place of all. It was there that George came up with the idea of joining the Navy. So here we are. *I* belong again and *I* am the one who is shielding his eyes to look at the wonders of a strange world.

The only source of discontent in my life at the moment is moving towards us. Abraham Seeley is a brute. He is a large, rough man with a straggly beard and a receding hairline. His teeth are brown and decayed and he always has a long clay pipe full of the foulest smelling tobacco clenched between them. A north country whaler like so many of the crew, Seeley seems to take pleasure in bullying anyone weaker than himself. I just catch a glimpse of him out of the corner of my eye before his thick, hairy hand slaps the back of my head and sets my ears ringing.

"What are you two lazy louts doing here staring into space? There's work to be done below. Get to it."

"We're just watching the mountains," I say, the words escaping before I can stop them.

"Talk back to me, will you? I'll teach you manners, you street urchin."

One of Seeley's huge hands grabs the back of my collar, the other holds George. Almost lifting us off our feet, he turns towards the hatch-cover. I know a beating is coming. Bitterly, I regret giving Seeley the excuse he was looking for.

A figure moves forward and blocks our way. The man is taller than Seeley, almost six feet, and he wears the uniform of the Royal Marine soldiers who are present on every Navy ship. Both his height and his manner give the impression that he can handle himself in trouble. He has a curly beard and black hair which has receded to show an ugly-looking scar running across his forehead.

"Leave them boys alone, Seeley," his voice is quiet but firm. Seeley hesitates.

"There's work to be done and they talked back. I was just going to teach them a lesson."

"There's no work needs doing right now." The soldier doesn't move an inch. "Let them be."

Seeley hesitates as if contemplating a response. Then, with a mumbled curse, he lets us go, pushes us harshly to the deck, and slouches off. The tall man helps us up.

"You boys keep clear of that one," he says. "Seeley's trouble." He stops talking and coughs harshly into a grubby handkerchief. Recovering quickly, he continues, "If he bothers you again, come and tell me. My name's Bill Braine."

With that he turns and pushes his way across the crowded deck. George and I return to the rail. My ears are still ringing, but at least we escaped a beating and are still in the fresh air, not below in the damp darkness and clutter of supplies, surrounded by the smell of cramped bodies and the scuttering rats.

"One dark night," says George quietly as we look out over the scattered, glittering ice floes, "that devil will find himself over the side in the freezing water." This is some consolation, but it is just bravado. This is Seeley's world and not the London streets; it is going to be a long voyage with him as our enemy.

Just then we hear a hoarse, panicked shout. "Look out below!"

Instinctively, we turn and look up. One of the sailors at the top of the mainmast has slipped. He is suspended by one hand from a sail rope as his companions scatter out of the way below. With horrible fascination we watch as he hangs thirty feet above the hard deck, shouting for help. Another sailor is inching his way along the spar. He is almost there, reaching out a hand, but he is too late. With a last cry of terror, the sailor loses his grip and falls.

For a moment no one moves, then everyone rushes forward. The ship's surgeon, Stanley, is close by and pushes through to crouch over the still form. After a brief examination he rises and shakes his head.

"Carry him below," he orders a group of men. "There is nothing we can do for him now but sew a shroud."

As the limp bundle disappears, the mood of the ship changes. Men clamber down from the masts in silence and go about their chores. Our first casualty has sobered us all.

I turn to go back below and feel Neptune brushing against my leg. He too has sensed the change. He seems to have taken to me and accompanies me at my duties whenever possible.

"Hello, old boy," I say softly, scratching his ear. "Let us hope that is the worst of our misfortune."

I am lying in a hammock, swinging gently to the rhythm of the ship. It is hot and stuffy and dark. The smell of unwashed bodies and burnt oil from the lamps is almost overpowering. My hammock is in a row of others, hung so closely together that we almost touch when we swing with the roll of the ship. Any space on the floor is stacked with crates of supplies and equipment, making it almost impossible to navigate in the darkness. And it is always dark between the decks. The only fresh air comes from the small hatch at the top of the ladder leading up to the deck, and it is usually kept closed. The only light comes from the foul-smelling hanging lamps. They smoke and sputter, but give little more than a dull glow.

The heat is unbearable. It is supplied through a system of pipes which run from our steam boiler. It is nice not to freeze, but the alternative is to suffocate and to suffer the continual drip of condensation from the walls and deck above. The warmth also encourages the rats which swarm over everything, eating anything they can get their teeth into: shoes, socks, furs. Periodically we must evacuate to allow a foul mixture of sulphur and arsenic to be burned to drive them off and kill them. It does make a difference for a while, but soon they are back as plentiful as before.

In spite of the other inconveniences, my hammock is comfortable. I have learned how to relax into its shape. I have even mastered the art of holding the stub of a candle in one hand and a book in the other. In this way I have been devouring the ship's library. My reading skills have improved to the point that I no longer need George's help or the lessons which the officers are giving those of the crew who wish to improve themselves.

I have finished reading now. Apart from the snores and grunts of a lot of men sleeping close together and the creaking of the ship's timbers as she pushes on, it is quiet. I am just thinking how strange all this is when I hear a voice close to my ear.

"Don't you ever talk back to me again," it threatens.

I don't even have a chance to turn before I am falling. I crash onto the pile of supplies on the deck below. My left arm painfully catches the corner of a crate and I cry out. All of a sudden there is a confusion of noise: shouts, curses, and yells.

From above George's voice calls, "Davy, what just happened?"

The end of my hammock is hanging free in the dim light before me. It has been neatly sliced through with a sharp knife.

"Someone cut through my hammock," I call back. I know who, but I will not say with all these men listening.

"Then sleep on the deck and shut up," a voice calls out of the darkness.

Carefully cradling my sore arm, I crawl into the most comfortable spot I can find among the crates and try to ignore the rustling of the rats close to my ear.

As things settle down again, I feel a warm shape nestling in beside me.

"Neptune," I whisper, "I guess I'll be sharing *your* bed tonight." Together we drift off into an uneasy sleep.

CHAPTER 7

The dreams were coming thick and fast now and I was losing the distinction between that world and my own. A tremendous gap was developing between my days and nights. During my waking hours I went through the motions of my "real" life. I didn't really care what happened. I was continually getting into trouble at school for not paying attention, not to mention my falling grades and incomplete assignments. In hockey I was spending a lot of time sitting on the bench because I was missing passes and shooting the puck as if the entire end zone were the goal. The only place where no one seemed to notice my preoccupation was at home. Mom and Dad were so wrapped up in their own problems that they didn't seem to notice me. But they did hear me.

One night while we were having dinner, I was thinking about the hammock dream I had had the night before.

"What?" asked my Dad, breaking the silence. He sounded puzzled. I must have looked confused because he continued, "You just said, 'I'll be sharing your bed tonight.' What did you mean? Whose bed?"

Slowly it dawned on me that what I had said to Neptune in the dream I had said out loud while I was remembering it.

"Nothing," I said hurriedly. "It was just a dream I had last night. I was remembering it and must have spoken out loud."

My Dad looked unconvinced and I was afraid he was going to ask me more about the dream. It wasn't that I was consciously keeping the dreams a secret, but to tell the truth I would have to tell the whole story and I didn't want to do that, at least not then. Fortunately, Mom spoke first.

"What's the matter with your arm dear?" she said in a worried tone. It was only then that I realized that I was rubbing my arm where I had struck the crate when my hammock was cut.

"It's nothing," I repeated. "I just banged it at school today."

That seemed to satisfy them and we lapsed back into silence. But the incident worried me. The dreams were becoming too real. My arm was not sore where I had hit it in the dream but, like talking out loud without noticing, my massaging it seemed to suggest that my dreams were beginning to impose themselves on my daily waking life. Maybe they were not just a story my mind was making up while I slept. Maybe there was something suspicious about them.

I was beginning to worry. After the dinner table incident, I resolved two things. Firstly, to be more careful about what I let slip in front of other people. I might get away with saying something dumb in front of my parents, but the guys at school wouldn't let me forget it so quickly and the last thing I wanted was a reputation for being weird or talking to myself.

Secondly, if the dreams persisted, I would have to talk to someone about them. They were just too strange to dismiss and perhaps they meant something. I didn't want them to stop but, on the other hand, I didn't want to "go crazy" either. For the moment though, I would wait and see where they were leading me.

The next day, Jim came to visit. He didn't get into town much, especially in the winter, so I guessed he had come to see me. When I got back from school, he was in the kitchen with Mom. They didn't hear me come in.

"Sometimes I wish he was interested in the farm. Then we could move out and be close to you." Mom sounded tired.

"The farm's been good to me, but it's not the life for everyone," Jim responded. "How are things between you?"

There was a pause before Mom answered.

"Not good, Jim. The business isn't doing well and that adds a strain. I think it's affecting Dave too. He's been really quiet and withdrawn the last few days."

I didn't like the turn the conversation was taking. Next, Jim would begin talking about my dreams and I didn't want that. I dropped my bag loudly in the hall and went into the kitchen.

"Hi, Jim," I said as cheerfully as I could.

"Dave, you're back," Mom said as she stood up. "Is that the time already? I have to go out and get some groceries for supper. I'll see you later, Jim. I won't be long."

Kissing me on the cheek, a habit I have never been fond of, Mom picked up her bag, put on her coat and left. Jim looked up at me from his seat at the table.

"There's some tea in the pot," he said. "Should still be hot."

"No thanks," I said, but I did grab a pop out of the fridge and sat down.

"So, how are you?" Jim asked.

"Fine," I replied.

"Any more dreams?"

"A couple," I said as casually as I could manage. Then, to move the conversation away from them, I talked about my reading on Franklin.

"I can't believe how dumb those guys were. McClintock said that the boats Franklin's men were dragging weighed hundreds of pounds and were full of useless junk like cutlery and curtain rods. They could never have made it across the Barren Lands with all that stuff."

"If that's where they were going."

"What do you mean? They left a note saying they

were going there."

"Not exactly." Jim took a sip of tea. He was settling into a story. "The note of 1848 says only that they are going to Back's Fish River. People have always assumed that they were going to continue south from there across the Barren Lands to try to reach a Hudson's Bay post. But Crozier and Fitzjames weren't stupid. They had Back's journal with them. They knew how impossible that trek would be with over one hundred sick men."

"So what were they trying to do?" I was being pulled into the story despite myself.

"Hunt. They probably had scurvy and the only way to cure that is to eat fresh food. Both Back and Simpson talk of the abundance of wildlife at the mouth of the Fish River. If they could restore their health, then they could return to the ships and escape when the ice broke up that summer."

"So why didn't they?"

"That is a very good question. We know some of them returned to the ships, because Irving's grave was found there and he was alive when they headed south. Re-manning the ships also explains the apparent junk they took with them. They didn't plan to travel with the stuff, it was cached against their return in case the ships sank.

"In 1848, they probably sailed at least one of the ships south. No one will ever know exactly what happened, but Inuit stories talk of survivors alive as late as 1850."

"Why didn't they adopt Inuit ways? Later explorers

did."

"Yes, but for Franklin's men it wasn't possible. There is no evidence that they even met any Inuit in the early years, and even if they had, the total indigenous population of the area was probably less than that of the crews. If they had tried to live there, it would have put an intolerable strain on the hunting and both Inuit and sailors would have died. Perhaps at the end one or two did meet up with the Inuit and live with them for a while, but they didn't make it back to civilization."

We sat in silence, contemplating the lonely fate of Franklin's men.

"But surely they could have been smarter and adapted more?" I said finally. "They seem to have been very inflexible."

"In some ways they were, but don't judge them by the standards of today. The technology simply wasn't there. The Victorians didn't send a man to the moon, not because they were dumb, but because the technology didn't exist. Suppose when Neil Armstrong stepped on the moon that his lander had broken down and the only way he could escape was to drive one of those little moon buggies over the Sea of Tranquillity. If the buggy is not suitable for the terrain, he dies. Suppose we then discover moon creatures who have specialized vehicles for moving easily over the moon's surface. Would we then call Neil Armstrong stupid for not adapting to ways he knew nothing about?"

Jim poured himself another cup of tea while I

thought about that.

"Making clothes from Caribou hides, or catching seals through the ice are very complex skills that take years to learn. Franklin's men did the best they could. Sure, they made mistakes, and they had more than their share of plain bad luck, but I very much doubt if an expedition today, placed in the same location and given the same resources as Franklin, would fare any better.

"Anyway," Jim continued, looking at his watch. "I have to head off now if I want to get home before it gets too dark. I don't drive as fast as I used too."

Jim stood up and stepped toward the door. Then he turned and looked at me.

"Dave," he said. "If you ever need to talk, about anything, not just the exploration, you know where I am. Okay?"

"Yeah," I nodded. "Thanks."

CHAPTER 8

It is Christmas and we are in the ice off Beechey Island, three months into our first winter in the Arctic. George and I are sitting on some tea chests finishing our Christmas dinner.

"Well, Davy, it was not the feast of the ghost of Christmas Present, but it was better than biscuits, bread and salt meat."

To mark the occasion we have all been given some of the eight thousand cans of Goldner's Patent Preserved Meat and some of the canned soups and vegetables that are normally reserved for the officers and the sick.

"Yes," I agree, "it tastes well enough, but I almost broke my tooth on that lump of solder in the meat. And I hear that some had to be thrown out because the cans were blown and the food rotten."

"True enough," answers George. "When we return, Mister Goldner will get no more Navy contracts. But a change in taste is as good as any banquet, as they say, and it is certainly better than black bread soaked in London drain water."

George looks at me and I cannot help but join in his laughter. Things have certainly improved for us since those days on the street. Later there will be theatrical entertainment and Lieutenant Gore will give a recital upon the flute, but for now everyone is content finishing off the meal and the extra tot of rum we have been issued. A sailor is hard at work on the hand organ in the corner and Jacko, who turns out to be Miss Jacko, is dressed in a blanket, frock and trousers made for her by the crew. She stands atop the organ and dances wildly to her favourite tunes.

Even Neptune seems content now, sitting at my feet, well-fed on scraps. This is unusual since he has been miserable ever since we left England. He mopes about getting in everybody's way or sits sullenly watching us all go about our work. The night the ice blocked us into our winter harbour here at Beechey Island, he sat on deck howling mournfully for hours and getting on everyone's nerves until I dragged him down to the mess deck where he lapsed into soft whimpering. It is strange behaviour.

"Well," says George, standing, "I think I will go and find a game of cards. Will you join me Davy?"

"No," I reply. "Cards are not to my liking. I think I may read some."

"You read too much. Come and have some fun."

"Do you remember who it was that taught me to read?" I ask.

"Aye. Well, maybe that was a mistake," George's voice suddenly becomes harsh. "You have become altogether too serious of late. I play cards for fun and if I can line my pockets with a few extra pennies for when we return, so much the better."

With that, George turns and finds his way over to some men who are huddled over a barrel against the far wall. I cannot deny it any longer; my friend is changing. The longer we are at sea, the less he reads. I have finished all Mister Dickens' books and have read many of the journals of the earlier explorers. I have tried to share my discoveries with him, but all he seems interested in doing is playing games of chance with his new friends. I am beginning to feel lonely. Reaching behind me, I bring out a copy of Lyrical Ballads by the poets Coleridge and Wordsworth. It is my first taste of poetry and much of it I do not understand. One poem however, "The Rime of the Ancient Mariner" by Mister Coleridge, tells a good story. I open the book at random and my eye falls on these lines:

And now there came both mist and snow,
And it grew wondrous cold:
And ice, mast-high, came floating by,
As green as emerald.

And through the drifts the snowy clifts

Did send a dismal sheen:
Nor shapes of men nor beasts we ken–
The ice was all between.

The ice was here, the ice was there,
The ice was all around:
It cracked and growled, and roared and howled,
Like noises in a swound!

I close the book and stand. A few men are still finishing off their rum. I do not care for it and find my way over to where Bill Braine sits. He continues to guard us against the menacing Seeley, although George needs him less and less as he spends more time with his card-playing friends. I have seen Bill and Seeley in conversation and am sure that Bill is repeating his earlier warning. Despite that, Seeley continues to torture us at every opportunity. After he cut my hammock, I managed to avoid him for a time, but that has become less easy now that we are stuck here in the ice.

"Here Bill," I say handing him my rum. "I have little taste for this stuff."

"Thank you," he replies, turning from his conversation with three other Marines. "Will you join us lad?"

"No," I answer. "I think I will get a breath of air."

As I turn to the ladder I see Seeley glowering at me from a corner. I hurry up onto the deck.

It is cold and quiet up here. There is little to see. It is overcast and misty and there are few lights on our ship.

About half a mile away, I can barely make out the dim lanterns of our sister ship, the *Terror*. It is a lonely world we inhabit. I had expected that, and the cold, but not the noise. I had imagined the icy landscape as immobile and silent, but it is not so. The ice is always on the move, driven by hidden currents in the sea beneath. It groans and grunts and creaks and roars as it is driven against itself and the nearby shore. It is just as Coleridge described. Huge blocks are pushed up into the air in jagged peaks and crash down in a tumult of broken shards. Were we not in a protected bay, the waves of pressure that pass through the ice would crush our two reinforced vessels as if they were made of paper. We are safe, but the power of the ice is frightening nonetheless and we are all aware that we are at the mercy of the elements.

The worst of it is the boredom. Unless I am going on one of the hunting trips, explorations, or to take magnetic readings, there is precious little to do. Every day that the weather permits us, we must exercise by running around the ship and by doing chores to keep the vessels and our shore camp shipshape. The officers have also organized numerous classes in reading and writing, a shipboard newspaper, *The Beechey Times*, and many theatrical productions. Even with all this, there is a lot of spare time. Every day I thank George for teaching me to read so that at least I can lose myself in the world of books. My only concern is that, if we must spend several winters like this, I will not have enough books to keep me going. Still, for the moment, that is not a problem.

There is also another sort of loneliness weighing on me. We are locked in the grip of an empty land and all of us miss the society of home, but I never expected George to be lost to me. More and more, his spare time is spent in the company of a group of younger seamen, joking and gambling at dice and cards. In the busy streets of London we were inseparable, but here, thousands of miles from civilization, he has all but deserted me. I have no other friends here, except perhaps for Neptune, who continues to keep me company much of the time.

I am so lost in thoughts of my loneliness and the ice that I do not hear the footfall behind me. All at once I am pushed painfully against the rail and a horribly familiar voice rasps in my ear.

"What do you mean by giving your tot of rum to that damned soldier Braine?"

I cannot answer for the pressure of the rail against my chest, but Seeley continues anyway.

"It's not friendly at this season of the year, and anyway, I'd have much more use for it." Seeley turns me roughly around to face him. I draw in a deep breath and manage to gasp, "What do you mean?"

Seeley's laugh is harsh and cruel. His mouth, just inches from my face, reeks of stale rum and tobacco.

"You don't know?" he sneers. "The rum won't do your friend no good because he's dying. He has the consumption. Have you not heard that cough of his? Soon he'll be coughing blood, if he isn't already. Then he's into the sick bay and from there it'll be a cold coffin for him my boy. Then who'll look after you and your cheeky friend?"

The shocking news sends a shiver down my spine which has nothing to do with the cold night air.

"You're lying," I shout and lash out with my foot. But Seeley avoids my blow easily and just laughs.

"You think so do you?" he asks. "Well, you listen carefully to that cough. There's others with it too—Hartnell in sick bay and young Torrington over on the *Terror*. They feed them the best food but it won't do no good. Some say as how they're coughing up bits of their lungs already. Won't be long till we're out there on that island digging two holes in that damned frozen ground, and it won't be long 'til there's a third one for Braine. You remember that, boy, next time you got some rum to go sharing out. You remember who'll still be around when your friend is six feet under."

With a last laugh, Seeley pushes me back against the rail, turns and disappears into the darkness. It can't be true! Yes, Bill has a cough, but most of us do, living in these dank quarters filled with the smell of the clay pipes everyone smokes. Bill's cough sounds deeper than some, but that doesn't mean that it's consumption. Seeley is just trying to scare me and get an extra tot of rum. Still, I feel uneasy as I rejoin the festivities.

The cliffs of Beechey Island loom over Neptune and me like a huge wall threatening to crush our puny bodies like ants. Below us, the white carpet of snow stretches away and becomes lost in the chaotic jumble of ice blocks. Out in the bay, all but invisible in the white wilderness, our two ships lie tilted at crazy angles like toys which have displeased a petulant child. Their decks are covered with canvas and walls of snow blocks protect their sides from the wind and almost hide their iron-clad hulls. Their position is marked most obviously by the large dark stain which covers the snow for a distance in all directions. Across the bay, the matching cliffs on Devon Island show black against the snow.

Below us, and clearly visible in the cold air, are the tents and buildings of the shore party, our cache of cans, and the flickering flame of the forge where William Smith and Samuel Honey work making nails and iron sled runners. Also visible, slightly back from the camp, is a small party of men working to break the frozen ground. It is April, 1846, and they are digging a grave.

"Well, Neptune." The dog looks up at me with his sad eyes. "Seeley's prophecy was true enough. Old Bill did have the consumption and now he will never leave this island. But at least he won't be alone in this bleak place. Seeley was also right about Hartnell and

Torrington."

I know it's silly but I feel the need to talk to someone and, these days, Neptune is the only one who will listen.

"Why did Bill hide his illness? Why did he go on that sledding trip to the magnetic camp? He could have said he was sick and stayed here. Maybe it was because Mister Fitzjames says the magnetic work is very important and will add valuable information which our scientists need to understand this strange phenomenon. Maybe he thought that by denying his illness, it would go away. Maybe he knew his own end was near and didn't want to give in. I don't know what it was Neptune. All I know is that I miss him.

"Eight men, seven haulers and an officer pulling a loaded sled over the ice. It is grueling work for fit men; it is brutal work for the sick. And Bill was already coughing blood, he could easily have been excused. I even tried to persuade him not to go the night before he left. Do you know what he said?"

Neptune cocks his head to one side.

"He said that he had to go, that it was what he came up here for. He even said that the walk in the fresh air would do him good. He told me to keep clear of Seeley 'till he got back."

Cold tears are coursing down my cheeks now. Neptune leans his big, friendly head against my leg as if to comfort me.

"Ten days they were gone and Bill only lasted six. Then they had to tie him to the sled. I knew, as soon as

I saw the hauling team was one man short, what had happened. Pneumonia, that's what Surgeon Stanley said, but in combination with the consumption, there was no hope. Poor Bill. He was raving like a madman when I visited him in the sick bay, talking about home as if he were there. Funny thing though, just as I was leaving he went quiet. I turned and he was staring at me with those sunken, fevered eyes of his. Then he said something I shall never tell anyone but you. He said, 'I am sorry I shall not finish this adventure with you, but I will rest easier in my coffin than you will on this ship. We should not have come to this bleak land and I shall not be the only one to stay. You will walk a lonesome road before you escape the frightful fiend who dogs your footsteps.' Then he fell back on his pillow. The next day he was dead.

"I don't understand what he meant. Perhaps it was just a symptom of his madness, but it sent a chill through me that I still haven't shaken off. You are my only friend now, Neptune. Bill is dead and George is more involved with his new friends than ever. Despite the fact that I am surrounded by over fifty other people, I am beginning to feel a loneliness creeping over me which scares me more than I can say. This voyage is not the adventure I thought it would be when we sailed from England a year ago."

As I scratch behind Neptune's ear, I watch the small party of men below us continue their struggle to break the frozen ground.

Breakup! An open lead of water has snaked into our little harbour and set us free. At least, it has set the *Terror* free, but it is only a matter of time before we too are able to sail again. All is chaos. We must rush to get our remaining supplies and equipment aboard. Fortunately, the scientific teams have already been recalled and we do not have to wait for anyone else to return. It will be difficult to leave Bill in this lonely place, but the exhilaration of moving again after so many months trapped in the frozen sea is overwhelming. And what's more, it is my birthday, June 23, 1846. I am thirteen. An early lead through the ice is my present. Surely with this gift, we will complete the passage and be home by the time I am fourteen!

Already the men are out with the ice saws cutting a channel through to the open water. Everyone is ecstatic to be on the move again. Even Neptune is wandering about the deck wagging his tail. George has come over and thrown an arm around me.

"The adventure continues Davy boy," he says with his familiar mischievous smile. It is just like old times. "Mind you," he goes on, "this lead has come at an awkward time."

"How so?" I ask. "Surely it just increases our chances of completing the passage this year."

"Yes," he agrees, "but it has cost me a good pair of

gloves. I wet them yesterday working on melting ice for fresh water and left them on a rock to dry. In all the confusion I completely forgot them. Maybe some other poor adventurer in years to come will visit this place and find a use for them. It is no matter; I will be so famous when we get home that I will be able to buy a hundred pair."

The cocky smile widens and we are brothers again. But there is no time to savor it. There is too much to be done if we are to take advantage of this opportunity.

CHAPTER 9

For all my fascination with the dreams, they scared me. Not just because the tension was beginning to mount, but because I had never heard of anyone else having a series of dreams as consistent, and persistent, as mine. Was this how madness began? Was my unconscious mind trying to tell me something by dredging up some long forgotten memory? Or was it just an insane fantasy put together, as Jim had suggested, from pieces of stories I had heard years before? I began to wish I could tell someone about all this; someone who would understand my dreams, be able to explain them, and reassure me that I wasn't going mad. I craved the dreams but, the longer they lasted, the more I worried about what they could mean. I was becoming lonelier all the time, cutting myself off from friends at school and growing more distant from my parents. The loneliness was beginning to frighten me. I had to talk to someone, but who?

I chose Mom for a number of reasons. No one at school would understand, my Dad was too preoccupied with his business to give me any time, and I had already tried talking to Jim. Mom had always had an interest in dreams. Dream therapy was one of the many things, along with pottery and Thai cooking, that she had taken classes in. I think she took courses to get away when things with Dad got too intense.

"It's not natural," she said when I told her how vivid and frequent my dreams were and how they seemed to be telling some kind of story. "I've never heard of anything like that before."

This wasn't very comforting, but Mom did have one idea—she suggested I see her therapist in Saskatoon. He was her response to the latest crisis with Dad.

"Chris might really be able to help," she said. "He is very sensitive to all kinds of issues."

At first I was reluctant to go, but Mom said that Chris was up on the latest theories about dreams and could help me understand what was going on. Anyway, it was worth a try and I was glad for a chance to get out of Humboldt.

The therapist's office was on the second floor of a low building downtown. It had a small reception area with a single secretary and one door with the words, "Chris Penner, Family Therapist" on it. I don't know what I expected to find behind that door, perhaps a leather couch, certificates on the wall. There were a few certificates, but no couch, just a couple of comfortable-looking chairs. One complete wall was a window that looked out over the town and made the room bright and cheerful. There was also a desk in front of the window with a bookcase on one side. In the back corner there were a couple of large cushions and a box of children's toys and picture books.

Chris ushered us in, sat down and chatted for a while about nothing in particular. When he started asking about the dreams, Mom answered for me until Chris gently suggested that she wait outside. I told him about the dreams and, to my relief, he seemed genuinely interested. When I had finished, he told me a bit about the importance of dreams in his line of work.

"I am not a psychoanalyst," he said, "but dreams have always interested me and I have found them useful in therapy sessions.

"First of all, your dreams are nothing to worry about. People used to believe that dreams signalled mental instability, but we dismissed that idea long ago. In fact, dreams are perfectly normal. Every mammal, except, oddly enough, the duckbilled platypus, dreams every night. Humans are in "dream sleep" for about two hours a night and have about five dreams in that time. That's almost one hundred thirty thousand dreams in an average lifetime. It's a shame we don't remember more of them.

"Anyway, no one has determined exactly why we dream. It might be to stimulate brain development, or to replenish chemicals in the brain, or to help sort and store the information we gather during the day. Some researchers even believe that dreams are used to erase unneeded information, rather like deleting unwanted files on your computer hard drive. Whatever their purpose, they are not caused, as my grandmother used to tell me, by eating too much cheese."

Chris smiled before continuing.

"The big question is, do they have meaning? Some say yes, that dreams are messages from our unconscious self and that we should take them seriously. Others say they are just random impulses from deep in the brain and that they mean nothing. I'm not sure who is right, but dreams do seem to reflect issues in real life, so perhaps they are an attempt to resolve problems which are bothering us when we are awake."

"Resolve problems?" I interrupted. "How can dreams do that?"

"Well, if something is bothering you, you tend to think about it all the time. But your rational, waking mind might be too preoccupied to see the answer clearly. The dream process, which sorts through the information without these preconceptions, might just come up with the answer.

"Now, these don't have to be emotional problems; they could be anything, even a school assignment. There is a story about a famous geologist called Louis Agassiz. He studied fossil fish from all over the world. Once he collected a beautiful specimen which was very complete and well-preserved. The problem was that it was not clear; he could not distinguish details which should have been obvious. For a long time he puzzled over why this should be until one night he had a dream. In the dream he saw the fossil fish and watched as a surface layer was peeled off to reveal the perfect skeleton. The next morning, he took the specimen and gently chipped at it. A thin layer of rock fell away to reveal the missing detail below. His dream had solved the problem that had been bothering him.

"There are many other examples of this process; writers, poets and artists often dream a story or a poem. It's not magical; it's just that they have been thinking a lot about their particular problem and the dream process resolves their conflict while they sleep."

"But how does that explain my dreams?" I asked quietly. "I'm worried that I might be going mad."

"No," Chris assured me. "Your dreams are definitely not a sign of madness, those kinds of dreams are very different. Your dreams are unusual in that they are very vivid and consistent, but they are still nothing to worry about. I think with some work we will be able to find out what is causing them. If you would like to come back next week, we can go into that more. In the meantime, why don't you write down your dreams as soon as you wake up. Then, later on in the day, read them over and underline any parts which are obviously related to something that happened the previous day or even something you may have heard or done in the recent past. If you bring that along next week, we can look at it together. It might give us some clues as to what these dreams mean."

"OK," I agreed as Chris stood up. "I'll do that. See you

next week."

We shook hands and I left. On the way home, I told Mom what had happened. She was a bit concerned at first, especially because Chris had asked her to leave, but I managed to reassure her that he had been really helpful. He had actually given me a lot of interesting information and certainly put my mind at ease. What I wasn't sure about was whether he would be able to explain what was happening any better than I could. Like Jim, he seemed to think that the dreams were old memories being processed. I was pretty sure they weren't, but I would try to do what he said before we met again the following week.

That night I went to bed relaxed and expectant. I even had a notebook and pencil on my table. Nothing happened. I slept a long time and when I awoke the next morning I felt refreshed, at first. But, gradually, I began to realize that, if I had dreamt anything, I could not remember it. Almost instantly, sadness flooded over me. I was almost in tears. What if the dreams didn't come again? I couldn't stand that. What if I never saw George or Neptune again? Confused and upset by my violent emotions, I stumbled through the day, hoping that the dreams would return that night, but again I was disappointed. I felt lost and terribly alone. I hadn't realized how involved I was in the dreams and how much I wanted to know what would happen next. Without them I was desolate. It was like coming to the end of a mystery novel and finding the last page ripped out, only a thousand times worse. I was a character in this novel and I would never know what happened to me. The whole week was a disaster.

My second session with Chris didn't go well at all. I had nothing to say and all he could do was repeat the same stuff he had said the week before. He speculated on the dreams' cause and why they had ceased. In some strange way, I blamed Chris for the loss of the dreams and that made me uncooperative. I didn't object when he suggested I leave early.

I didn't feel any better after the session, but I had some spare time so I went to the library to pick up a book on Franklin I had ordered the week before. It was a journal written by one of the officers from the expedition that had discovered Franklin's first wintering site on Beechey Island. It was pretty dull and only told me stuff I had read a dozen times before. There were descriptions of the three graves of John Torrington, John Hartnell and William Braine, the foundations of the blacksmith's workshop and the pile of discarded cans. As I thumbed through it I began drifting away. I was thinking that there was not much point in going to see Chris again. Then my eye caught something. It was a brief footnote that I could have easily missed. It discussed the possibility that the ships had left Beechey Island in a hurry. That in itself was not remarkable. What was, was that one of the searchers had found a pair of gloves laid out to dry. They had been weighed down with a rock and forgotten in the haste to leave.

I was stunned. George's gloves, left behind in the

rush to take advantage of the open lead. It was a detail of my last dream that I could not have known from anywhere else. It was as if George were trying to talk to me. He was sending me a message: *Don't listen to anyone else. Only your dreams are true. No one else will understand.*

Maybe there was hope yet! Maybe my dreams would come back. I tucked the book under my arm and rushed out to meet Mom in the car. I told her I wasn't going back to see Chris again. I put it very positively, saying he had been a great help, but that there was no point now that the dreams had stopped. On the drive home we chatted about school and sports, but my mind was in turmoil. I couldn't keep my eyes off the book. I was convinced that, in some way, that footnote was a message from George and I was almost too scared to hope that it meant that the dreams would return.

That night I dreamt again. This time I told no one. But I did follow one of Chris' suggestions—I wrote the dreams down. Not for him, but so that, if they stopped again, at least I would have something concrete to remember. The dreams were mine, and I was not going to risk losing them again until they had led me to the end, whatever or wherever that might be.

CHAPTER 10

In nine days I will be fourteen. What a difference it will be from my last birthday when we left Beechey Island with such high hopes. Then I thought that we would be celebrated heroes by now. Instead, I am standing by the rail looking out over a grey wilderness of ice and snow. Neptune sits by my feet. He is my constant—my only—companion these days. I cannot help remembering what a difficult year it has been.

At first progress was slow as the ice was still heavy. Often we had to wait for an open lead heading in our direction, then we would cautiously follow it until we could go no farther. Twice the *Erebus* became trapped and we waited nervously to see if we should escape. Then, at last, we reached Cape Felix, the northernmost tip of King William Land.

This is where we are now, halfway between east and west and farther than any man has gone by ship before. A few miles south of us is the cairn at Victory Point built by James Ross at the end of his sled trip from the east three years before I was born. Only sixty miles south of that is another cairn. This one was built only seven years ago by Simpson and Dease on their canoe journey from the west. That sixty miles is the last unexplored bit of the Northwest Passage. It seemed when we first arrived that our success was assured.

It was late summer but there was still a full twelve hours of light each day. The west coast of the island was blocked by heavy ice, so we set off down the east side, down Ross Strait. The bottom of the strait was unexplored, but we hoped it connected to Simpson's Strait and we could sail around King William Land. The ice was light and progress was good. It looked as if we would easily reach Simpson's cairn. But half way down the shallows beat us. After days of trying to find deep enough water to continue, the *Terror* grounded. It took a week and the removal of many supplies to refloat her. The stores we stacked neatly on the beach; who could say if we might have need of them one day? Then, sadly, we sailed back north to search for a way through the heavy ice to the west. For weeks we tacked back and forth following blind leads and watching the frozen waves of ice heave restlessly. Finally, on September 12 last year, both ships became beset and we resigned ourselves to a second winter frozen in an icy stranglehold.

As I stand here lost in my thoughts, I can hardly distinguish this last winter from the one before. Both are little more than a haze of cold and boredom. Seeley spent much of the time away from the ships, so I was happy enough with my books. I am now big and strong enough to take part in sled hauling and I did manage a few short trips to visit our scientific camps. The main magnetic camp is set up at Cape Felix on King William Land. It must be on land since the sea ice moves. The work is of the most boring sort and consists of sitting watching a pendulum and a dip needle and recording their movements every hour. There must be no metal nearby and even our belt buckles must be removed for fear that they will interfere with the readings. What we discover will be of great interest since we are a mere hundred miles from the location of the Magnetic North Pole which James Ross visited in 1831.

Surgeon Stanley has become very adept at skinning and preserving birds and now has a sizeable collection. His assistant, Goodsir, is kept busy collecting and drawing all manner of creatures which he obtains with a dredge through holes in the ice. As our supplies are used, the extra space is soon filled with specimens and we continue to gather information at every opportunity.

George has returned to his gambling ways and we grow farther apart. This Arctic loneliness affects us all in strange ways. I find that I am withdrawing more into myself while many of the men become more querulous and rowdy. There have been a number of fights, and knives have been drawn, although no one has been seriously injured yet.

With the coming of spring and the end of the

winter storms, it was decided that two sled parties would set out to map King William Land. One would go down the west coast and complete the Northwest Passage. The other would work down the east and explore that region. Lots were drawn and we were all elated when the *Erebus* won the honour of completing the passage. On the 24 May, 1847 Lieutenant Gore, Mate Charles Des Voeux and six men set off on their historic journey. We all envied them and heartily cheered them on their way. Simultaneously, but with less enthusiasm, Lieutenant Little and Mate Robert Thomas led a team from the *Terror* in the opposite direction.

Both parties have been away nearly three weeks now. Mister Gore's team was to move fast and he is expected back any day now. They were heavily laden with supplies to begin with, but planned to drop provisions at depots for future parties. As soon as they reached Simpson's cairn they were to return. Mister Little's trip is longer. He is expected to be away for some time yet. If there is no word of him by my birthday, we will send out a party to meet him.

As I gaze out on the colourless vista, I sense a presence behind me. Dreading that devil Seeley catching me unaware, I jump round. The figure in front of me is not Seeley, but almost as frightening.

Sir John is no longer a young man, and the voyage has taken a toll on him. He always appears confident and cheerful in front of the men, but he has lost weight and seems almost to be sagging under the burden of leadership. His face has taken on something of a grey pallor.

"Good day lad," Franklin smiles faintly at me, "I did not mean to startle you. Are you keeping watch for Mister Gore?"

"Aye sir," I stammer nervously. "His will be a great achievement."

"It will be that." The smile broadens. "To complete the passage is what we came for. But it is our scientific work that will live on long after our journey is forgotten. This stretch of water is of no use for commerce." Sir John turns his gaze out over the ice. "I have spent many years in these lands. I have seen men starve and have almost died myself. No one will willingly come here with any hopes of profit. The only force strong enough to compel men to suffer in these latitudes is the desire to learn. To know what this world, so different from our own, is really like."

Franklin falls silent and I have not the courage to interrupt his thoughts. Eventually he begins speaking again, but more to the barren wastelands than to me.

"It is a perilous journey we have undertaken and I have been plagued by black dreams of late. I see a lonely grave and I fear that it might be my own."

I am horrified that Sir John, who has been the strength and driving force for us all, should be thinking this way. But I am too terrified to offer any comfort.

"That day we first met," he says, "when I had that damned image made, I was suffering mightily from a cold. That very evening, I drifted into uneasy sleep on the couch beside the fire. My dear wife Jane was beside me embroidering the Union flag which I am to raise on the completion of the passage. I felt a weight on my legs and awoke. I found the flag thrown over me for warmth. Poor Jane, she did not realize that the Union Jack is only draped over a corpse."

After a moment's silence, Sir John seems to shake himself from his sad reverie and turns to me. "Do you still have your companion?"

It is a strange question and I try to answer as best I can. "George is below. He will be cleaning the...."

"No," Sir John manages a wan smile as he interrupts me, "I recall when I first saw you that I was getting two sailors for the price of one. Is that still true?"

"Aye sir," I reply, understanding at last. I pull Jack Tar from my pocket and hold him up. "Here he is."

"Good lad. Keep him warm now, he is not dressed for these climes. You have another friend too I see." Franklin reaches down to scratch Neptune's ear. A shout from the topmast stops him.

"Sled on the ice. South south east."

Sir John straightens. "It seems Mister Gore is back." With a last half-smile he turns and walks across the deck. He has only gone some ten paces when he stops. As I watch, his broad back seems to tense. He takes another half-step and stops again. One knee buckles and the large figure slumps to the deck.

For what seems like hours no one moves. Then Mister Fitzjames, who is coming down the bridge ladder, jumps the last few steps and rushes over. Soon there is a crowd around the fallen figure. Surgeon Stanley is called and Sir John is carried below. I am in a turmoil. What has happened? Will he be all right?

It is night and I am in my hammock, but I cannot sleep. It has been such a day of contrast that I do not know what to think. First Sir John spoke with me. Then he collapsed. Within hours Mister Gore and his party were back with the news that the Northwest Passage has been completed. He is rushed to Franklin's bedside. The great man has regained consciousness, but he is paralyzed down his left side and only occasionally aware of his surroundings. He is alert enough to realize the significance of Lieutenant Gore's achievement and promptly elevates him to the rank of Commander. It is almost his last act. Within the hour he lapsed into unconsciousness and, at ten o'clock this evening, Sir John Franklin died.

How could the heart of such a strong, noble man fail so suddenly? He had become the symbol of our endeavor. How could we fail with him at the helm? Now he is gone and we have yet another grave to dig. Although I only met him twice, his death only adds to my almost overwhelming sense of loneliness.

It is one of the few days recently when the cursed wind is not blowing through our bones. It has dropped to a gentle breeze, but still we huddle in the lee of the sled to hide from it. There are nine of us scattered around a small fire which engulfs the last fragments of our supply boxes. The fire is precious, for there is no wood in this land, yet the circumstances warrant it. Eight of us are a sledging party from *Erebus*.

George sits beside me. We are led by Captain Fitzjames who, since Sir John's death, is now second in command below Mister Crozier. Our aim is to meet with the *Terror* party under Mister Little. The ninth member of our sad circle is Henry Sait of that party. He sits across the fire from me. His cheeks are hollow and his eyes sunken and glazed. He is barcly able to keep upright.

We have been out for three days now. This morning Mister Fitzjames, who was out in front, shouted that he had spotted something. It soon resolved into the emaciated figure of Sait. He was staggering all over and, when we brought him in, incapable of recognizing any of us. He was mumbling incoherently and looked close to death. It is for him we have built the fire. Its warmth, and some biscuits and brandy, have revived him some-what. We are all eager to hear his story, although none of us think it will be to our liking. We lean forward expectantly as Sait tells his tale.

"At first we made good time," he begins hesitantly. "Of course, we were disappointed not to be completing the passage, but we made light of it and joked of what we might find on our side of the island. The land was bleak and flat and the jagged rocks which make up the beaches hereabouts made walking on the land difficult.

We found the going much easier on the sea ice where it was flat, close in to the coast. The only trouble we had was in traversing a long inlet which was packed with a jumbled mass of ice. It was tiring work and it took us two days to cover only ten miles. Mister Little named the inlet Hardwork Cove."

Sait's eyes lift to the horizon and he drifts off into some private reverie until Mister Fitzjames nudges him. Sait sips some tea and continues.

"There were some large islands offshore, which we took time to explore, but were of little interest. The coast continued southeast and the weather remained fair although the ice was becoming rougher and we had to go ashore frequently to pass open patches of water.

"After we crossed a large peninsula, our route turned southwest and we all felt we would soon be heading back up to the ships. We had reached our most southerly point when we were faced with a wide lead of open water. Since beach travel was so hard and as there was a collection of small islets offshore, Mister Little decided that we should head that way, examine the islets and try to pass the lead on the seaward side.

"We had barely gone halfway when a crack opened in the ice beneath us and the sled began to be drawn into the icy water. I was at the front and so I threw off the harness, but the rest of the men were pulled in. All managed to scramble onto the ice, but soaked to the skin and with no supplies, our predicament was severe."

Sait hesitates again as if drawing strength to tell the rest of his tale.

"We made camp on the closest island in a makeshift shelter of rocks and snow. That night, Mister Little, who had spent a considerable time in the freezing water trying to help men out and save some supplies, died. We buried him in the morning as best we could. Before we had finished, the wind was up and it was beginning to snow.

"It was not much of a storm, but it trapped us for five days. Five others died before the wind eased and Mister Thomas and myself could leave. We followed the coast for days, hoping to find a supply cache left by Mister Gore. We lost all track of time and my companion began to rave about his wife and family back in England. At last he fell. We were walking along a low ridge when he just lay down in mid-step. I went over to help him up and found him dead.

"I don't know how long I staggered on. I do not remember much until I found myself beside your fire."

Silence falls across our group like a shroud. Henry Sait sits gazing at the rocks at his feet and no one else feels the urge to speak. At last Mister Fitzjames says, "Set up the tents. We will camp here and attempt to find the body of Mister Thomas. Thank you, gentlemen."

"What is going wrong George?" I ask as we move over to begin unpacking the sled. "Our luck seems to have left us along with Sir John. Seven men dead and one so weak he may not last long. Will any of us get out of this God forsaken place alive?"

"Don't talk like that Davy." George is making an effort to lift my spirits. "It is bad luck all right, but remember the dove when we set sail?"

"Yes," I reply sadly, "but I also remember the man who fell from the mast—was that not an equally *bad* omen?"

"That was nothing. He got careless is all. You'll see. We're halfway there and still with supplies a'plenty to see us through. Come summer this damned ice will break open and we will be on our way home. It is a shame Sir John won't be able to take us, but Crozier's a good man. He knows the Arctic almost as well as Sir John and he will surely see us through."

"I suppose so." I know George is right; it is only a spell of bad luck, but I cannot get rid of the idea that things have changed for the worse.

"Anyway, let's get these tents up and some food made. I fear Mister Fitzjames will have some work for us to do come morning."

We bend to the task before us, but the pitiful image of poor Henry Sait staggering alone through this unforgiving wilderness hovers before my eyes. Will that be the end for us all? My mind will not let go of some lines from Coleridge's poem. They seem to echo the last words of my poor friend Bill Braine:

Like one, that on a lonesome road
Doth walk in fear and dread,
And having once turned round walks on,
And turns no more his head;
Because he knows a frightful fiend
Doth close behind him tread.

CHAPTER 11

The dreams were so real now that I hardly knew what was reality and what was not. In school I would drift off into recollections of the previous night and return surprised that the floes of shimmering blue ice were mere desks, the cliffs only blackboards and the grunting walruses simply teachers insisting on an answer to a question I hadn't heard. I just couldn't be bothered. The concerns of the real world seemed irrelevant compared to those in my dreams.

One day I was walking across the schoolyard with Wayne, one of my friends from the team. Sarah and a few other girls were walking toward us. I had never made any secret of the fact that I thought Sarah was beautiful, but she had never shown any sign of being interested in me. Her crowd was the school elite, and I was a long way from that social circle. As we passed, she looked straight at me, gave a smile that would normally have made my knees turn to jello and said cheerily,

"Hi, Dave."

I just kept walking.

When we were past, Wayne nudged me hard and said, "What are you doing? I thought you were crazy about her. Why didn't you stop and talk?"

I just shrugged.

"I don't know," I said. "I guess I didn't feel like it."

Wayne shook his head, "Man, you're getting really weird," he said and walked off.

The truth was, I really didn't feel like myself any-more. I was constantly thinking about my dream self. I really was getting weird. All I wanted was to sleep and dream. I stopped going out with my friends so that I could go to bed early. On weekend afternoons, I snuck away from whatever chore I had been assigned, curled up, and slept in an attempt to return to my other world.

Some nights would bring two or three short dreams, others just a single long, involved one. Either way they were always in order and always advanced the story. They also varied from simple images, which stood on their own, to complex dream-memories of things my waking self could know nothing about. Sometimes it even seemed like my dream self was keeping a sort of spoken journal. Whatever form my dreams took, every morning I could remember each one as if I had actually lived it.

I was becoming obsessed, and people were beginning to notice. Teachers commented and asked me if every-thing was okay at home. My parents asked if everything was all right at school. Even my friends gave me a hard time about never doing anything with them. But I didn't care; my dreams were everything.

But I couldn't ignore the real world entirely. One day I came home around supper time. I was just reaching up to open the door when I heard Mom's voice from inside. It was loud and she sounded upset.

"But we can't go on like this," she was saying. "You have to sell that business. It's not working."

I stopped and listened even though I had heard this before. Dad had tried everything at one time or another: selling cars, real estate, landscaping. They were all failures and it was always Mom who spotted it first. Dad tended to always look on the bright side and blame the economic climate or unreliable suppliers.

His latest project was running the local franchise fried chicken place. It's called Fingers 'n Wings. He even had a secret batter recipe. It should have stayed secret. The stuff tasted like cardboard and it had the texture of partly-set carpenter's glue. The guys at school laughed at the place and wouldn't be seen dead there. So the only customers Dad got were the little old ladies who came in on "Seniors' Wednesday" to gum their way through a few soggy fries and maybe a donut. Even they didn't try the secret batter. The chicken place was the worst of Dad's ideas, and right now it wasn't doing well.

"There's not even enough money coming in to pay our debts, never mind buy groceries and clothes," Mom continued.

"It needs a chance to build up a customer base. It's...."

"It's had three years," Mom interrupted, "and you still only get six people on a busy night. Face it, the chicken place is a failure."

That was the wrong word for Mom to use. I guess Dad felt she was calling him a failure and he got very defensive.

"I've built that place up from nothing," he shouted. "This town needs a place like mine. It's just a matter of time."

I heard footsteps coming toward the door and jumped back. The door flew wide open and Dad stormed past me as if I didn't exist. I went in. Mom was standing in the living room. Her back was to me, but I knew she was crying. I went to my room and closed the door quietly. I felt terrible. I was angry at Dad for making Mom cry. Sometimes the fights worked the other way around and then I felt angry at Mom for being unfair to Dad. The dreams were becoming more and more tense and now life at home seemed to be falling apart.

In the past, the fights had made me feel so helpless that all I could think of was running away. I never did, but I would lie in bed and plan how I would do it. I would plan what I needed to take with me, when would be the best time to leave so that they wouldn't find out, and where I was going to go. Eventually I would fall asleep and in the morning the fight would be over and the thought of going and living on the streets of Vancouver wouldn't seem quite so attractive. As I lay in my room this time listening to the silence, I began to think that escape was the answer, both here and in my dreams.

CHAPTER 12

"Mister Young, be so kind as to bring my box of pens and ink to the tent."

Captain Fitzjames is gesturing from the doorway of one of the large tents set up on a beach of jagged rock at Victory Point. Even this late in the winter, the endless, howling wind has swept bare the slightly higher places in this flat land. It has also sucked all colour out of the view. We exist in a world of monochrome; all is white or grey as far as the eye can see. In some senses, the land is more depressing than the sea. At least on the sea ice there are the pressure ridges to break the monotony. Were it not for them, it would be impossible to tell where the water ended and the land began.

Victory Point was named by James Ross as the farthest point west he achieved. It seems we shall get no farther either. It is April, 1848 and we have not moved in a year. The ice did not melt last summer and the ships are still locked fast. Food is plentiful but scurvy haunts us and many are becoming weak. Leg muscles are painful after the least exertion; gums bleed and teeth loosen for no reason. Our daily exercise does no good and the lemon juice is not sufficient to keep the disease at bay for much longer. We need fresh supplies to halt the ravages of scurvy, and there is no game in this God-forsaken spot, so we are going south to hunt. The journals of Simpson and Back talk of plentiful deer and partridge in these regions. Perhaps when we return the ice will break and we can continue.

As quickly as my freezing fingers will allow, I rummage through the boxes piled beside me. We have brought much of our equipment ashore, mostly from the *Terror* as she has been holed by the ice. If it should release its grip while we are gone, she will surely sink. The *Erebus* is in good condition and will serve us well if she can be freed. The supplies are piled all around, in places, higher than the tents. What we will take with us is already loaded into the seven boats which are set on runners to form sleds. Even with that number, and in our weakened condition, there are ample men to haul and we should make good time. Hopefully the worst of the winter storms are over. It is very cold and a brisk wind is blowing powdery snow against my legs.

I carry the small box over to Fitzjames and hold it out.

"Come in boy, come in. You might as well get out of the wind."

Inside the tent it is not much warmer than out, but at least I am sheltered from the wind. Two oil lamps swing gently from the cross pole, casting a dull, eerie glow over the huddled figures. The tent creaks and flaps quietly in the wind.

Captain Fitzjames takes the box and sits down at the small, makeshift desk. Captain Crozier, the commander since Sir John died, sits opposite. On the floor to one side sits Lieutenant Irving, weary from his trek to the cairn from which he has retrieved Lieutenant Gore's message from last year. We will add to that note in the unlikely event that someone should come by in our absence. I don't wish to go back outside and no one orders me to leave, so I sit quietly in the corner and watch. Fitzjames begins the laborious process of thawing the ink.

"Well Irving," Crozier turns to the young Lieutenant on the floor, "was it a hard trek to the cairn?"

"Not too bad sir," Irving replies, "but I must admit to feeling the effects somewhat."

"Yes, none of us seems to have the stamina of old. It is this damned salt meat. I could kill for a good roast pheasant and a decent glass of claret. Still, with luck, in a very short while we shall be feasting on fresh venison. God willing, that will restore our strength." Crozier stops talking and lets his gaze drift to the nearest oil lamp.

"Six officers dead this past winter and no cause that the doctors could find. Certainly there was some scurvy, but it is worst among the men and not yet bad enough to kill. With Little, Thomas and Sir John that makes nine officers in all. Why? We keep the most active and eat the most tinned food. We should be in the best of health. And yet the officers seem to get sicker than the men. The worst is poor old Gore. He should have lived to savor at least some of the glory of completing the passage." Crozier drifts off into his own silent reverie. It is interrupted by Fitzjames.

"The ink's ready now sir."

"Very well," Crozier pulls himself back with difficulty and begins to dictate slowly. "Twenty-fifth April 1848 Her Majesty's Ships *Terror* and *Erebus* were deserted on the twenty-second April three leagues north-north-west of this." Crozier hesitates. "No, that should be five leagues north-north-west of this," he pauses while Fitzjames makes the change, "having been beset since twelfth September 1846. The officers and crews consisting of one-hundred-and-five souls under the command of Captain F. R. M. Crozier landed here—put in the latitude and longitude here Fitz."

There is a moment when the only sound is the scratching of Fitzjames' pen. Then Crozier continues.

"This paper was found by Lieutenant Irving in the cairn."

"Sir," Irving interrupts, "it was under the cairn, not in it."

"Very well, make it under the cairn—*under the cairn supposed to have been built by Sir James Ross in 1831—where it had been deposited by the late Commander Gore in May 1847. Sir James Ross' pillar has not, however, been found and the paper has been transferred to this position which is that in which Sir James Ross' pillar was erected.*"

We wait in silence again as the pen finishes its scratching.

"Read it back Fitz."

After Fitzjames has finished reading, changes are made. First Irving adds something, "Sir, the cairn was four miles to the north, perhaps we should say that."

"Yes," says Crozier. "Put that in Fitz, after 1831. And while you are at it change May to June. Now we must add the sad news. *Sir John Franklin died on the eleventh June 1847 and the total loss by deaths in the expedition has been to this date nine officers and...*how many men Fitz?"

"Of all causes, fifteen in total."

"Right. Well, put that in and then sign it."

Fitzjames scratches his signature and passes the paper over to Crozier who reads it one more time and adds his signature.

"Should we say where we are going sir?" Irving puts in almost tentatively. Crozier thinks for a minute.

"If all goes well, we will be back long before anyone sees this note, but I suppose you are right." Crozier bends again over the document and says slowly as he writes, "*and start on tomorrow twenty-sixth for Back's Fish River.*"

Crozier puts the pen down, folds the document and passes it to Irving.

"Thank you Lieutenant. Be so good as to replace this and have the men rebuild the cairn."

Irving stands and pushes through the tent flaps. I am just about to follow when Crozier speaks again.

"So Fitz, what does the future hold for us now?"

"That is a hard question," Fitzjames replies. "If only the ice had broken last summer we should be home, or at least well on our way by now. I only hope the men are strong enough to get us to the hunting grounds."

"They will liven up when they see the game and have something to do," Crozier replies. "It is the boredom as much as the illness. Three years on board ship in this bleak wilderness is enough to make any man sick. But what then? We have but three options. We can head through the Barren Lands for a Hudson's Bay post, traverse Boothia for Ross' supply cache at Fury Beach and wait there for a whaler, or return here in hopes that the ice breaks this year and we can sail on in the *Erebus*. I fear the old *Terror* will go no farther."

The two men fall silent. The only sound now is the lonely, mournful wail of the rising wind. Fitzjames' eyes drift down to the corner where I sit huddled.

"Boy, you are still here. What do you think? Which way should we go once our bellies are full of fresh meat?"

They are asking me? For a moment I am speechless.

"Go on," Crozier encourages, "tell us what you think."

"Well sir," I begin tentatively, "I have read George Back's narrative of his journeys in the Barren Lands and on the Fish River. As he describes it, it is a desperate place with no food or shelter. I fear we would find little to sustain us there."

Both the officers are watching me intently and smile encouragement.

"On the other hand, the supplies left by Ross may well have been taken by whalers or locals. If that is the case, we would be little better off for our long march to Fury Beach and not able to await the uncertain arrival of whalers. The *Erebus* is still in good shape and, if needs be, we could spend a further winter on her. But if the ice should break up, and surely it cannot hold us forever, then she would be our fastest and surest way back home. I feel that, with our strength restored by fresh food, we would be best advised to return here and attempt a passage later in the year."

I fall silent, amazed at my temerity. But they do not seem in the least put out by my musings.

"Well put boy," says Crozier. "I see you have not wasted the long hours of darkness. We think alike. Stay in the Navy when we get home. I warrant you'll make an officer in the end. Now go and get some rest. We have a journey ahead of us and you will need strength for it. Fitzjames and I will consider your advice."

As I struggle back out into the biting wind, Neptune shuffles over and falls into step beside me.

"Well old boy," I whisper, "you won't believe me, but I have been giving advice to the commander and it is in line with his own thoughts."

Neptune lifts his head and looks up at me with sorrowful eyes as if to say, "Good for you, but I hope you are both right."

The dog and I have become inseparable. In one sense, he has taken the place of George. I reach down to scratch his ear. When I stand, Seeley is there before me.

"Been telling tales to the officers have you boy?" he sneers. "We ain't good enough for you with all your fancy book learning."

Neptune, who has developed a strong dislike for Seeley, growls deep in his throat.

"And that filthy beast," Seeley continues. "He's scrawny enough but I reckon there is enough fresh meat on him for one good stew."

Seeley aims a kick at Neptune and catches him square in the side, bowling him over in the snow. I leap forward and swing wildly, catching the unprepared Seeley full on the jaw. As much in surprise as from the force of the blow, he falls to the ground. It is the opportunity Neptune has been waiting for. In a flash he is on his feet and lunging for Seeley's face. His teeth sink into Seeley's left cheek and the man screams. Flailing madly he tries to escape, but Neptune holds his grip. Shouting at the top of my voice, I grab Neptune's collar and manage to pull him away. Blood covers Seeley's face and is splattered on the snow. He struggles to his feet.

"That damned dog's dead," is all he says as he staggers off to find the surgeon. Neptune, what have you done?

The single shot seems to echo forever across the bleak landscape. My tears are hot, but they freeze in the wind before they are half way down my cheeks. I pleaded with Fitzjames, but it did no good. I pleaded with George, but he just shrugged; what could he have done anyway? I even pleaded with Seeley, but he was merciless.

Seeley stands nearby, watching me. The left side of his face is heavily bandaged, but enough is showing to let me see that he is smirking. He was as good as his word. Neptune is dead and I am more alone than ever.

CHAPTER 13

The morning after Neptune died, I awoke crying. I hadn't cried in years, yet here I was lying on a soaking wet pillow over a dream. My dreams were changing. The sense of companionship and adventure was gone, a huge black cloud was hovering above me. But I had to see them through to the end and, though I still craved the nights and the stories, their sadness lingered throughout the days. Of course, I couldn't blame all my misery on my dreams. My parents' problems were also getting worse.

I felt trapped. I would lie in bed at night and listen to them shouting at each other through the wall. I worried that the fights would get so bad that they would split up and then what would I do? Sometimes I wanted to scream at them to shut up. Why were they doing this?

Around the time I dreamt that Neptune was shot, Mom and Dad's fights began to get worse. In the past, they had always tried to hold off until I was out of the room. It didn't make much difference, but at least it gave me the opportunity to slip out of the house unnoticed if things got too bad. Then I would go and hang out at the mall or the video arcade for a few hours until things had calmed down. But that day Mom didn't hold back. She tore into Dad for all his mistakes right in front of me. I think he knew deep down that she was right, but he couldn't admit it out loud. Pretty soon they were screaming at each other about something that happened years ago and had nothing to do with the stupid chicken place.

Watching them go at each other was just too much. Something snapped inside me. The pressure that was building up from the fights and the dreams was overwhelming. I yelled at them to shut up and stormed out of the house.

I only went down to the arcade for a couple of hours, but I guess it made them feel bad. When I got back they were both really apologetic. Things settled down and we even began talking about where we would go for a holiday this summer. Dad suggested we go down to California, but Mom gave him one of those looks which means, "We can't afford that."

"We could go camping," she said. "Out to the coast, or maybe even down to Oregon. The beaches are nice there and we had a great time when we went three years ago."

Dad nodded.

"Yeah, that would be good. Just the three of us in

the tent trailer. I could get away for a couple of weeks."

Mom shot Dad another of her looks. This one meant, "You had better."

That was when I screwed up. I didn't realize how important it was to them. Sure I had enjoyed the holiday three years ago, but I had only been eleven then. Now, my idea of fun wasn't a tent trailer in Oregon with my folks, and I had already arranged something else. I should have told them long before this, but the dreams had me so preoccupied that it had just slipped my mind. Wayne's parents had a cabin by a lake south of Saskatoon and I was going there for the last half of the summer. There was lots to do there: water-skiing, swimming, wind surfing, and lots of other people my age. In fact, Sarah's parents had a cabin on the other side of the same lake. So I told them I couldn't go to Oregon. It was lousy timing, and they looked really hurt. They didn't say anything, but late that night I could hear them arguing again through the wall. Finally, I went to sleep, and the dreams took over.

CHAPTER 14

The flowers are beautiful. The ground is a flat carpet of yellow and red. There are still patches of snow in the hollows, but now small streams run here and there at random. The air seems full of birds of all different kinds. Most incredibly, the horizon is a single moving mass of life: deer (reindeer the whalers call them) in a single moving river of brown bodies. The sound is like a low groan as thousands of hooves rise and fall on the soft ground. It is interspersed with a low clack as the antlers of the male deer knock together. It is almost impossible to believe that this paradise of life and colour can exist so close to the dull world of black and grey we have been inhabiting for so long.

The deer are so thick that they are difficult to hunt. Small groups of men are scattered all along the edge of the herd waiting for an animal to stray off. When one does, there is invariably a sharp musket crash and a scuttle of activity as it is dragged clear and cleaned.

Behind me, makeshift racks are already full of meat hanging in the weak sun. The Commander was right, the men have livened up with the activity and fresh meat. It is almost enough to make me believe that all will be well in the end.

"Well, this is better than that rat-infested hulk," George says, standing beside me watching the scene. It is summer, 1848. "We should have come down here long ago. Damned officers don't seem to know what they're doing."

"I don't know George," I reply defensively. " Mister Crozier and Mister Fitzjames seem like good men. In any case, this game won't stay here forever, and then we will be better off back in the ships."

"Davy! You have been listening to the high-and-mighty's too much. You never used to pay no heed to old Marback, and now its *Mister* Crozier and *Mister* Fitzjames. They only care for themselves and their good life. We have to look after ourselves. We always have and we can't change now. Anyhow, things are going to be different around here soon and you had best be sure you know which side you're on."

"What do you mean?" But it is too late, George turns on his heel and is already several steps ahead.

"We're not going back to rot for another year on those God-forsaken hulks of yours." There is a general murmur of agreement at Seeley's words. The cuts on his cheek where Neptune bit him have scarred, but they are still a livid red and give his face a twisted look. "You officers and any men who ain't got the guts to stay can go if you want, but the rest of us is staying here. Right boys?" The murmur turns to a low roar which sweeps through the ranks of men standing on the shore beside the stretch of water we have named Plenty Bay.

"This is mutiny," Crozier's voice is colder than the chunks of ice floating in the wide bay behind him. "It is also stupidity. The game will not stay here forever and then where will you go? Will you walk to Canada over the Barren Lands or perhaps swim Baffin Bay to seek shelter with the natives of Greenland? Your best chance—our best chance—is to return to the ships and, when the ice frees them, sail the *Erebus* home through the passage as we were ordered to do."

"And if the ice don't free her?" Seeley has taken a step forward and is looking hard at Crozier. "What if the ice crushes her? Then you are stuck where there ain't no game at all. I say stay here where at least a man can eat fresh meat. If they don't come to rescue us this summer, they'll come next for sure."

"Seeley, you're a fool." Crozier says it calmly, but the men tense at his words. "And you men are fools as well to listen to him. The game will be gone when the first snow falls. You cannot store enough now to see you through the winter and you don't have the native's skills to catch seals on the ice. You'll starve long before any help arrives. The officers and I, and any men who wish to come are taking two sleds and returning to the ships. Those who stay will be charged with mutiny when we return to England. Any who try to stop us will be shot."

The men behind Seeley look restless and uncertain as Crozier's small group handle their muskets.

"Let them go," Seeley almost commands the men, "and any who wants to join them can. I for one ain't going back for a fourth winter on those hellish ships. Soon enough these boys'll be back begging us for some fresh meat and then we'll see who's going to be charged with mutiny."

"Will anyone else join us?" Crozier asks the crowd behind Seeley. A few men look uncertain but Seeley's hard eye travels over them and no one comes over. I look hard at George standing in the front row and try to will him to come over. But he is firm, not even looking in my direction.

So we turn and set off. Fifteen officers and twenty-three men dragging two boats over the peninsula and back up the island to what we hope are the waiting ships. Only time will tell us who is right and who is wrong. Will I ever see my friend George again?

Our small group stands along the rail of the *Erebus*. It is July 1849 and I have been sixteen for a scant three weeks. At last, after three winters in this place, we are in free water once more. What should be elation and joy are tempered by the sight before us.

It is one of the saddest things in the world to see a ship sink. Especially one which has been so much a part of one's life for so long. The ice is loosening its grip on the poor, holed *Terror*. The old ship who began her life fighting against Napoleon has served us well. But now she is going to rest. She lies heeled over a full thirty-five degrees and her masts are broken. The ice cracks and groans and roars as it reluctantly sets her free and she screams a last farewell as her timbers, broken by the pressure of years, are painfully released. We watch in silence as she slowly tips farther over. Now the bow is sinking and the blunt stern is being slowly forced up into the air. A sudden, horrible noise announces that the boiler has broken free. With frightening rapidity now, the poor ship rises almost to the vertical and sinks below the dark, cold water. Nothing remains except a few supplies discarded on the ice around that awful black hole.

But we do not have time to mourn. We too are free, and our ship is unholed, so we must make the most of it. There has been some discussion about retracing our route north back through Lancaster Sound into Baffin Bay, but that would mean abandoning what men may be left at Plenty Bay. As Captain Crozier said, "They may be mutineers, but they are still my crew and I will not abandon any of them who wish to come with us."

So we will continue on the route fate has mapped out for us and which we began so long ago with such high hopes. Perhaps it is open all the way through and we will still sail out in triumph to Alaska. But it will be a hollow triumph at best after all that has befallen us. I do not want to think of George or of what may await us at Plenty Bay, so I busy myself with the tasks at hand.

I can see the tents from the rail but, fortunately, the frightfulness of that camp is hidden by the distance. What a cruel jest the name Plenty Bay seems now.

The shore party found three men. Three men from the sixty-seven we said farewell to last year, and they too sick with scurvy to move. They are a sorrowful sight. They are swollen and covered with sores. They can barely move their limbs for the pain and their teeth may be pulled free with ease. Most strange, they bleed freely from wounds which healed years before. They have been brought on board and tell a tale we can hardly bear to hear.

True to Captain Crozier's prediction, the game vanished with the first snow. At first they still dined well on the preserved meat and the provisions we carried down with us, but as the weather grew worse and the supplies grew short, sickness broke out and the men became weak. A party took three boats and attempted to return to the ships. We will never know what happened to them.

As the horrible winter wore on, Seeley became more and more crazed, berating even the sick for getting him into this predicament. To disagree with him was enough to earn a beating or even worse. Eventually the food ran out. Some of the men went mad and ran about screaming until they dropped. Others gave up, lay down and stared silently into space until they too died. Still others, led and organized by Seeley, resorted to a more frightful means to stave off death—they ate the remains of their comrades.

As soon as the worst of the winter storms abated, Seeley led a group of survivors, no more than thirty half-starved men, east in an attempt to reach the whaling grounds. The three men we found were too sick to go and had been part of a group left behind to die. That would have been their fate in a very short time had we not come along.

Our way too is clear now. We have come down here through uncertain passages and leads, but the ice has closed firm behind us. There is no way back and we must go on now regardless. Seeley and his devils must fend for themselves as best they can in the wilderness. And George, where is he? Did he join the unfortunate party who perished attempting to return to the ship, or did he stay at camp and die here, or is he somewhere out there with Seeley, still alive?

This is the end, we can go no farther. The *Erebus* still floats free but, as far as the eye can see there is impenetrable ice. We know the way back is blocked so there is only one option left to our small party—Simpson Strait. If we can sail through it we may still be able to cross to the Gulf of Boothia and meet up with whalers before 1849 is out. We must, for another winter will be the death of us all. It will be a hard journey in our weakened state, but better than trying to cross the Barren Lands.

The problem is that the strait is too shallow for the *Erebus* so we must abandon her and take to the small boats. They are loaded now and we are hauling on the oars looking back at the *Erebus* where she sits, calm and peaceful, at anchor in a flat open sea. On our left looms the mainland shore of the Adelaide Peninsula. On our right the bleak, hopeless rock of King William Land which has become a grave to so many of our friends. Will it be ours too before this hellish journey is over?

CHAPTER 15

By this time, my dreams had become like a horror movie that I was compelled to watch. Every night I was drawn back, fascinated, to the story created by the dark imaginings of my overwrought mind, but I did not want to follow where they led. The sense of loneliness was almost overwhelming and it took an enormous effort of will even to get out of bed in the morning.

After the holiday disappointment, Mom and Dad's fights just kept getting worse. It seemed like they argued every day and it didn't matter whether I was around or not. When they weren't actually arguing, they were bickering at each other. The pressure began to build again.

It was Friday night and their third fight of the week. I was watching TV and they were going at it behind me.

"That place is like an albatross around our necks," my Mom was saying. "You have to get rid of it."

"No," my Dad shouted. "I have to give it a chance."

"You've given it a chance. It's not working."

It was the same old stuff as before. Their voices were mingling with whatever I was watching on TV.

"Look." Mom was trying to calm down and try a different approach. "I can get a job. Dorothy says she needs some help at the store. It wouldn't pay much, but it would help us over this spell. But I won't do it to support the chicken place. We have to get out from underneath that."

"All I need is more time." Dad was still being defensive. "I know it will work out."

"No it won't," I hadn't planned to say anything, it just came out. I certainly hadn't planned to take anyone's side. "Dad, no one is going to go there. The place is a joke. My friends wouldn't be caught dead there. How many people under sixty do you see there in a week? Without a younger crowd, it doesn't have a hope."

There was an uncomfortable silence while both my parents looked at me in amazement. Mom was about to say something, but Dad got in first. He was furious.

"What do you know about running a business?" he screamed. "It's damned hard work, and I do it for you. You're just some ungrateful, smart-assed kid who should learn to keep out of other people's affairs. You can't even get decent grades in school any more. All you do is hang out with that no-good bunch of layabouts. You should get out and get a job."

I had had enough. My anger got the better of me.

"Well, at least it's better than being a loser that

everyone laughs at," I shouted. Before I knew what I was doing, I was on my feet and heading for the door. With every step, I expected to hear a shout. I expected, no I wanted, him to come running after me. But he didn't. He never said a word and the silence when I closed the door was worse than anything he could have said.

I felt I was the only person in the world. That was why I didn't go to the mall, hang out for a few hours, and then sneak back in after they had gone to bed. That silence had scared me.

It was almost dark, and it was the middle of February. All I had were the clothes I wore and the baseball jacket I had grabbed on the way out, and it was beginning to snow. It wasn't how I had planned to run away. Then I had an idea—Jim's place. I hadn't seen him since the time he came around to visit. He had dismissed my dreams in the past, but a lot had happened since then. Perhaps now he would believe me. In any case, he would give me a bed for the night and I wouldn't have to listen to the shouting through the wall.

I walked down to the highway and stuck my thumb out. I didn't have to wait long (the advantage of a small town). A truck soon stopped for me. It was an old farmer I'd seen a couple of times at the market. He was driving a beat-up 4x4, but the cab was warm.

By the time we got to Jim's road, it was snowing pretty hard and the old guy warned me about the storm. He wanted to know where I was going dressed in such a light jacket. I told him it wasn't far and I'd walked it a hundred times, even in winter. He still wasn't happy, so I pointed out some lights that we could just see through the snow and said that was Jim's place. It wasn't, but there was no way I was going to let this guy stop me.

Eventually, he let me out but he sat there for the longest time, I guess until he couldn't see me any more. I made as if I was heading for the lights and then, when I heard him drive off, I turned back onto the dirt road.

It seemed a lot colder than it had been in town, but I figured that was just because it was dark now. I was soon wishing I had grabbed my down parka. The baseball jacket was beginning to seem awfully thin. The snow was getting heavier too, and was already drifting in the ditches. Still, I wasn't worried, all I had to do was follow the road until I came to Jim's mailbox.

By the time I recognized the carved squirrel, it was snowing so hard that I couldn't see Jim's house. In fact, if I looked down I couldn't even see the ground in front of me. I guess it's what's called a white out. It was like being wrapped in a huge, soft, white blanket, except that there was no warmth. My feet and hands had gone numb and I was so cold I had even stopped shivering. The only reason I found the mailbox at all was that I was staggering along holding onto the fence beside the ditch. It meant wading through the drifts which was hard work, but in the centre of the road I could have been walking through downtown Saskatoon for all I could see. Plus, I couldn't keep to a straight line and was always stumbling into the ditch.

Anyhow, I had found the mailbox. Now all I had to do was find Jim's front door.

I'll never know how I missed the house. When I left the mailbox I was walking straight towards it and it couldn't have been more than fifty metres away. Even in a white out I was sure I could walk straight for that far. But I couldn't. Once I missed the house the first time I was completely lost.

I kept falling over fences and banging into broken-down walls. Once I was sure I had found the house, but it was just the side of the old ramshackle barn and as soon as I left it I was lost again. By the time I stumbled over the pigsty I was getting pretty scared. Jim hadn't kept pigs for years, but I crawled in anyway just to get out of the snow. Then a funny thing happened, I began to feel warm. It was still twenty-five degrees below zero and there was still a blizzard raging, yet I felt warm. So warm that I could curl up and go to sleep. I'd sleep the storm out and then I'd find the house in the daylight. I crawled into the corner and pulled my knees up. The snow was blowing through cracks in the wood, but it didn't seem to matter. I was warm and my eyes were getting heavy.

The most mournful sound in the entire world is the flap of a heavy canvas tent in a biting Arctic wind. It is as if the devil is snapping a towel at your heels. And the devil must have played a large part in this disaster.

How could so much hope turn to such tragedy? I thought my life was beginning anew when George and I escaped from Marback's....

Mister Fitzjames is now only occasionally conscious. I have wrapped him in as much clothing as I can find, but he is still frozen. I fear he will not live long. This storm will be our last. When it hit, our boats were exposed in shallow water. We were through Simpson Strait and near the mouth of the inlet which leads to Back's Fish River. But we couldn't stay together. The last I saw of Crozier's boat it was being driven out to sea and the men in it were fighting to keep it from being swamped. We seemed to derive more shelter from a spit of land and were not in such serious difficulty. But still Mister Fitzjames was having trouble keeping us level. The waves were breaking high over the gunwales and we had to bail continuously to keep from swamping.

"We must try for a beach to see this out," Fitzjames could barely be heard above the wind although he was shouting at the top of his lungs.

With all the white water around, we could see little and could only hope that the water would calm as we proceeded up the inlet. At least the wind was driving us in the direction we wanted to go. But it was driving us too fast and we did not see the reef until the jagged rocks crashed through the bow. In an instant we were all in the icy water.

Fortunately there was a beach nearby and four of us managed to crawl up onto it. It was rocky and inhospitable, but better than the water. Equipment and pieces of boat were washed up all around us. One man was badly hurt and died before we could get a tent up. The three of us huddled here and waited for the end. The following day the other man died. He just let out a sigh in his sleep and that was it. I managed to drag him outside and now it is only Mister Fitzjames and myself sitting huddled here as the devil torments us.

Mister Fitzjames is sometimes delirious and talks of his sister Elizabeth back in England. He clutches a journal he has kept for her these many hard years and which she will never see. At least I have no one to worry about back home. I should like to know what happened to George though. I sit and clutch the cold form of Jack Tar.

The devil is getting braver. He is fumbling with the tent flap. It must be time for him to come in. He has it open now.

Why does the devil have George's face?

This is strange. How can George be looking into my tent? I see now. It is George and the devil is behind him, pushing him hard into the small, wind-battered space. George falls across my legs. The devil pushes the flap aside and comes in. The scars on his left cheek twist his features into a horrible grin. The devil has Seeley's face.

"George?" My mind seems to be working very slowly. "Is that really you? You don't look well." George's face is impossibly thin. His cheek bones stick out and his eyes seem sunk far back in his skull.

"Yes, Davy," he replies. "It is me. A sorry state we have all come to now, eh?"

"What a touching reunion." Seeley is sneering across at us. He looks far better fed than my friend. I shudder as I remember why that probably is. "I see you are still with your officer friend. A lot of good it will do you now."

"How many are you?" I ignore Seeley and direct my question at George.

"Just us," George looks down at the floor as he answers.

"What happened to the rest?" I have to know.

"They died." George doesn't want to explain, but Seeley has no qualms.

"They died all right," he says almost gleefully, "and I helped a few of 'em along with this." He grins horribly and produces a long, evil-looking knife. "But some of the boys are still with us, ain't that right George? Loaded on the sled outside they are." Seeley throws back his head and lets out a hideous laugh.

"But don't you boys worry. You won't feel nothing and I'll make sure they build a nice big memorial to you all when I gets home."

"You're not going to get home Seeley." I have no fear left of this man. "None of us are. This is the end, the last camp. None of what you have done, or will do, matters any more. No one will ever know what happened to us or where or how we died. This place has swallowed us as if we never existed. Your petty insanities count for nought now."

Seeley seems confused by this. For a moment he sits looking at me with a puzzled frown. Then, raising the knife, he begins to crawl over the bedding towards me. I don't have the strength to defeat him, and I don't care. What difference does it make now how the last of us die?

Seeley is almost over me now. The knife is raised even higher.

"Elizabeth! Is that you? It is perilous cold, can you bring an extra blanket for my poor legs."

Fitzjames, in his sad delirium, has seen a figure moving. Sitting suddenly bolt upright, he grabs ineffectually at Seeley's clothes. Startled, Seeley turns and slashes down with the knife. It sinks deep into Fitzjames' chest. With a sigh, he falls back, half-pulling Seeley with him.

Suddenly I want to do something. Even if no one will ever know, I must not let the last act of this tragedy be Seeley's. Everything seems to be happening in slow motion; Seeley is struggling to regain the knife and I am fighting the heaviness of my limbs. The clothes and blankets feel like glue holding me back. Under my knees I can feel the hard, rounded shape of poor Mister Fitzjames' telescope. I don't know what I'll do when I reach Seeley. Nothing much if he gets the knife free before I get there. The knife is almost free now; I will not make it in time.

George has always been faster than me. In a sort of funny half-crawl, half-hobble, he claws his way past me and grabs hold of Seeley. The blow is weak, but it is enough to knock Seeley off balance; as he falls the knife pulls free. It is insane. We are possibly the last three people alive for hundreds of miles and we are trying to kill each other. George is trying frantically to get a grip on Seeley's wrist. The knife slashes wildly, catching George on the side of the face and ripping the clothes at his shoulder. He falls aside. I rise to my knees and swing the heavy brass telescope as hard as I can.

For a moment Seeley looks surprised. Then he drops the knife and puts his hand up to the spot on his forehead where a thin trickle of blood is running down from his scalp. He tries to turn and look at me, but the effort is too great and he slumps over in an untidy heap. The weight of his falling body is too great for the already strained tent and it collapses on top of us.

Is Seeley dead? I don't really care, all I want to do is go to sleep, but George is more alert. I feel myself being dragged from beneath the canvas into the cutting wind and snow.

"Leave me be," I protest into the wind, "I want to sleep."

"No!" the words are harsh even against the storm. "You must not. Get up, we will walk home."

I look up into George's face. One side is covered in blood and the whole is gaunt and hollow, but the eyes still have that sparkle.

"Come on Davy boy." The voice is the cheery one I remember from Marback's and from our readings in the cold, wet streets of London. If my friend George Chambers thinks we can walk home then we can. I will follow him anywhere. Painfully slowly, I struggle to my feet, leaning into the icy wind.

"That's it Davy, up you get. It's not far now. I'm going to save your life just as you and that old telescope saved mine. I've been lonely for a long time—all but a century and a half. But we're together now and this is my chance to repay you. You won't forget me now will you? Or the others? Tell our story Davy. It's been a long time hidden and needs told. Promise?"

I nod slowly.

"I knew you would. It's a good story isn't it? And we did have some adventures did we not? I don't think, despite it all, I would swap it for another meal of gruel at old Marback's.

"Come on, it's time to go. Take my hand."

George holds out his hand and I reach out to take it. It is cold, colder than the snow around us but I don't care. We are together again, just George and I, team-mates once more. George begins to walk through the blizzard. He walks backwards, never taking his eyes off me. I stumble along behind, holding that cold, cold hand. There is a light, behind George, getting brighter. And a doorway, leading to where? Without turning, George hammers his fist on the door. We stand together in the snow and wind, our eyes and hands locked. Then the door opens. A blinding light washes out, my legs give way and I collapse—into Jim's warm kitchen.

EPILOGUE

Several hours must have passed. I wake up wrapped in blankets before a roaring fire in Jim's livingroom. My feet and hands hurt, but at least I can feel them.

"Good morning," says Jim from the chair across the hearth. "I phoned your folks to tell them you were all right. They were getting pretty worried. You are one lucky kid. People have frozen to death in a blizzard, just a few feet from their back door."

"George showed me the door," I reply tiredly. Then I look round. "Where is he?"

"George?" Jim looks puzzled. "Who's George?"

"George Chambers," I say. Then it all comes back: the tent, the knife, the telescope, Seeley. George is just a dream. I blurt out the story of the tent and the pigsty. Jim sits silent and unblinking, picking up every word. When I am finished, he sits for a moment. Then he turns and calls down the hall, "Jurgen, come here please."

Hesitantly, a figure appears from the shadows into

the firelight and I gasp in recognition. It is a boy about my age. He was slightly taller than I with a thin face and deep-set brown eyes peering out from under an unruly mop of sandy-coloured hair. A large bandage covers his cheek and part of his forehead. He is dressed in dark, loose-fitting, hand-woven clothes, patched in several places. Shyly, he looks down at the floor.

"This is Jurgen," Jim is saying. "He is from the Hutterite colony down the road. It was he who found you in the sty and brought you in. He has been helping me around the farm and got trapped here by the blizzard. He was down at the barn checking on old Victoria. She gets upset and lonely in bad weather, so I rigged a rope line from the back door to her stall so I could check her even in a storm. Jurgen kindly offered to check on her this evening. He was following the rope back when he fell over you by the old pigsty. Gave himself a nasty gash on an old nail too. You were almost asleep and he had the devil's own job getting you to wake up and follow him to the house. I think you owe him your life."

Through all this I don't take my eyes off the boy and he doesn't move.

"Thank you," I say. "Thank you very much."

Jurgen lifts his head and looks at me for a brief moment. He says nothing, but the sparkle in those eyes is one I know very well.

"He doesn't speak much English," Jim interrupts our communion, "but with the little bad German I know, we get by. Danke Jurgen, you should get some rest now, schlaff."

Nodding silently, the boy turns and disappears down the corridor. I look after him for a moment then turn to Jim.

"That was who rescued me all right. But he is also George from my dream. How can that be? How can I dream about a person for weeks before I meet him?"

"I don't know," Jim replies thoughtfully. "The mind is a complex and poorly understood thing. Perhaps your experience in the blizzard imprinted Jurgen's image onto the dream image of George or perhaps it is just a coincidence that they look alike."

"Or perhaps," I interrupt, "he really is George and there is some supernatural link between the historical George of my dreams and Jurgen, who saved my life."

This time I am not going to let Jim pass my dreams off as wild imaginings. He sits for a long moment staring at me in the firelight.

"Perhaps you should tell me the whole story?" he asks eventually.

So I do. From the very beginning, I tell Jim everything. It is like a release. I feel like the ancient mariner in the poem, only able to rest after I tell my tale to someone. The whole story comes without any effort, and Jim listens to every word. By the time I have finished the fire is burning low. For the longest time Jim says nothing.

"You have an extraordinary tale to tell," he says eventually, looking at me thoughtfully. Then he asks, "But who is the dream George?"

"I don't know," I reply honestly.

"I think I do," says Jim.

I stare at him for a moment before he continues.

"When I came back from visiting you, I did some digging. I figured that if Franklin and Fitzjames were real enough perhaps George Chambers was too."

Jim leans over and picks up the book we had examined on my last visit. Flipping quickly to the back, he holds it open to me. The page is headed; Appendix 1: *Crew List The Franklin Expedition*. There follows a long list of names. My eye hesitates on the ones I recognize from my readings and dreams. Most are at the top of the list, officer's names.

Sir John Franklin—Commander Expedition
Commander James Fitzjames—Captain H.M.S. *Erebus*
Francis Rawdon Moira Crozier—Captain H.M.S. *Terror*
Graham Gore—Lieutenant H.M.S. *Erebus*
Charles Frederick Des Voeux—Mate H.M.S. *Erebus*
Edward Little—Lieutenant H.M.S. *Terror*
Robert Thomas—Mate H.M.S. *Terror*
Stephen Samuel Stanley—Surgeon H.M.S. *Erebus*
Harry Goodsir—Assistant Surgeon H.M.S. *Erebus*

There is also John Torrington—Leading Stoker H.M.S. *Erebus* and John Hartnell—Able Seamen H.M.S. *Erebus*, both dead of consumption and buried on Beechey Island beside my friend William Braine—Private, Royal Marines H.M.S. *Erebus*.

But my eye lingers longest on one name I have come to dread and fear over the last few weeks. The name of a man my dream-self has perhaps killed,

Abraham Seeley—Able Seamen H.M.S. *Erebus*.

It looks harmless enough as a dry fact sitting amongst so very many other sad names, but it will always bring horror to me whenever I see it.

I am gazing at Seeley's name when Jim leans over and gently turns the page. The list continues, and most of the names mean nothing to me, but one does. Right at the bottom is a name I had half expected to see, but cannot really believe is there.

George Chambers—Cabin Boy H.M.S. *Erebus*.

It is a shock, but what really sends the shivers down my spine is the fact that the *Erebus* had two cabin boys. The second one is David Young.

It makes sense; after all, I *am* a character in my dreams, but I never expected to see it here in black-and-white.

"It's me!" the exclamation escapes almost unbidden. Jim nods slowly.

"That proves my dreams are true!"

"Perhaps." Jim is speaking quietly. "There is certainly something strange going on here. You have dreamt of things you couldn't possibly know from reading. Whether they are true or imaginings, I don't know."

"They're true," I almost shout. Jim raises a hand.

"I believe perhaps they may be," he continues. "But what is true for you may not be true for everyone. Without a doubt you have experienced something remarkable, and if you believe it, surely that is all that really matters."

"Do you believe me?" It is important to me that Jim understands what has happened.

"Oh, I believe what you say. The problem is what it means." Jim pauses and looks at me thoughtfully. "There is one more thing I can perhaps add to your story. Do you remember the Navy button I gave you?"

"Yes," I say. "But it proves nothing."

"True," continues Jim, "But it was not the only thing I inherited." Slowly Jim rises and fetches a small box from the mantle. As he does so, he continues speaking. "I always assumed that this had nothing to do with my ancestor's trip up north. I thought it was merely a personal momento which had survived the ravages of time. Now I am not so sure. Take a look."

Jim hands me the box. My fingers are shaking as I open it. Inside the box, nestled on a bed of shredded paper lies a faded, worn lead figure. It is a toy sailor. There are only patches of white and blue paint left, but his hand is still held firmly over his eyes as he looks at some wondrous, exotic landscape.

"Jack Tar." I breathe the words almost silently.

"It would seem so," says Jim. "I have never shown this to you or to anyone else. I never thought it of any importance. I guess I was wrong. In any case, I think he belongs to you now."

The ancient figure fits comfortably into the palm of my hand. I close my fingers around him protectively.

"Thank you," I say. Neither of us need to say more. The story is told and George can rest now. But I cannot.

"My parents," I ask. "Were they mad at me?"

Jim looks at me hard. "No," he says, "not mad, but they were pretty worried with this blizzard coming on.

Maybe you should give them a call."

Jim gets up and moves the phone to the table beside me. It seems to ring forever. Then I hear my Mom's voice. "Hello?"

"Hi Mom, it's Dave."

"Dave." She sounds tired. "Are you all right? Jim called to say you were out there. How did you get there in the blizzard? We were so worried."

"It's okay Mom. I hitched out. I just got a little turned around in the yard. But I'm fine now. I'll stay here tonight and come home in the morning. I've got some stories to tell you."

"Yes." She sounds a little hesitant. "Your Dad and I have been talking, and we think we should all get together and discuss things. Anyway, there's lots of time for that. Your Dad wants to have a word. You get a good night's sleep, and we'll see you in the morning. I'm so glad you're all right."

There's a moment's silence while Mom passes the phone over. I'm so ashamed of what I said earlier that I almost put the receiver down, but then Dad's there.

"Dave. How are you?"

"Fine Dad. Look, I'm sorry I made you and Mom worry so much."

"That's all right. You're okay now and that's what's important." There's a pause and then he continues. "Listen, I'm sorry I laid into you the way I did. I'm pretty stressed right now. Your Mom and I have been talking. She thinks it would be a good idea if she and I went to see Chris. She might be right too. Anyway, we'll give it a try. We've also decided to put the franchise up for sale. I guess the economic climate isn't right just now." There is another pause, then he continues. "Anyway, we'll talk about all that tomorrow."

"Okay Dad." This is very difficult for me. "Listen, I'm sorry too, about what I said—I mean, before I walked out. I had no right to say those things. It was...."

"Never mind," he interrupts. I think he is finding this as hard as I am. "We'll sort it all out tomorrow. Right now you need to get some sleep. I'll come out in the morning, as soon as they get the highway cleared, and pick you up. Good night Dave."

"Good night Dad."

I hang up. I am so tired I can barely keep my eyes open. Jim has made up the spare bed for me. It is so comfortable, it is like sleeping on clouds. I feel more relaxed than I have in weeks. The dreams are over and my life can get back to normal. In the morning I will go home and resolve what I must with my parents. Maybe I'll even give Sarah a call.

I won't walk out again. When the right time comes, I will leave. I don't know what my own life will bring but I know now I will be able to handle it somehow. George has taught me that.

"Thank you," I murmur into the darkness.

Just before I drift into a luxurious, dreamless sleep, I imagine I hear soft footsteps outside my door and the whispered reply, "You're welcome, Davy boy."

THE END